INCOGNITO

Suzanne Allain

LeMoyne House

LeMoyne House, Publishers

Cover image courtesy of www.georgeglazer.com, George Glazer Gallery, New York City.

ISBN 978-0-9823682-4-4
First LeMoyne House Edition 2009

To my mother, my best critic
And my grandmother, my biggest fan.

One

☙ ❧

Lady Elizabeth Smithfield, relict of Sir John Smithfield, surveyed her two daughters as they sat together, their heads bent over their needlework. Lydia, her light brown hair picking up golden highlights in the morning sun, was dutifully working away at the laborious task, sewing small, intricate stitches that would eventually result in a pillow or seat cushion her mother could proudly display. *Sweet Lydia,* her mother thought, a gentle smile lightening her somewhat rigid countenance. Glancing over at her younger daughter, Emily, the smile disappeared and was replaced by a slight frown. Her needlework forgotten on her lap, Emily sat gazing out the window, softly humming a ditty her mother was sure she had not learned in a polite drawing room. It was probably fortunate Emily had ceased her stitching, if the few wide, uneven stitches were an indication of how the finished product would appear.

Lady Smithfield heaved a great sigh, wondering, as she often did, why her second daughter could not have been a younger replica of the oldest, or, better yet, a son. It was one of her frequent laments since she and her daughters had been forced to leave their home upon the death of Sir John two years previously. Since Sir John lacked a direct male heir, Rollings Park had gone to a distant cousin and his family, and the Smithfield ladies had been forced to relocate to their present, more modest domicile in Stonehurst.

The house they were able to purchase from a wealthy attorney was small but comfortable, with classical lines, a pleasing redbrick façade, and an interior said to have been designed by Robert Adam. However, Lady Smithfield felt their decline in the world quite forcibly. She was no longer Lady Smithfield of Rollings Park with a staff of forty and a full stable. In their less affluent circumstances, they could barely afford six servants and one carriage.

When Lady Smithfield sighed a second time, Emily and Lydia exchanged a knowing look that their mother did not see. They were well aware of the cause of their mother's melancholy. Emily tried to be sympathetic, as she missed Rollings as well, but she could not help wishing her mother's sighs were for Sir John rather than his estate. To distract her mother's thoughts, Emily motioned to the letters on the rosewood table and asked if anything interesting had come in the post.

Lady Smithfield picked up the morning correspondence and leafed through it in a halfhearted manner. One letter caught her eye, and, setting aside the rest, she scanned it eagerly. Upon discerning the nature of its contents, her gloomy manner dissipated completely, and her features took on a look of joy coupled with disbelief.

"My dears, I have just received a letter from His Grace, duke of Alford, with some very encouraging news!" Lady Smithfield paused briefly to ensure she had her two daughters' full attention. Confident they were listening, she continued, "You may remember, girls, that the duchess and I were schoolmates at Miss Finch's Academy for Young Ladies and that we remained friends even after we both married." Knowing her daughters had heard many times of their mother's friendship with the duchess of Alford—as had anyone who had spent more than half an hour in conversation with Lady Smithfield—she hastened to the point. "You might recall also that we both wished that you, Lydia, would marry Lucy's son, Lord Wesleigh. But when the duchess died, I felt my cherished hope would come to naught. But it is not to be!" She paused in happy anticipation of her daughters' reaction to the news, but as her announcement elicited confusion rather than excitement, she hurried to explain. "What I mean to say is, it is not going to come to nothing, it will proceed after all. The duke has suggested it himself! He writes that if we are in agreement with the proposal, an announcement of the marriage of Miss Lydia Smithfield to Lord Wesleigh will be inserted in the *Morning Post* in thirty days. My daughter, the future duchess of Alford. I can hardly credit it! I daresay this is the happiest day of my life." The joyful news moved Lady Smithfield to tears, and as she searched for her handkerchief, she missed the less-than-joyful looks her daughters exchanged.

Lydia, with her light brown hair, big blue eyes, long slender neck, and ladylike demeanor, was generally deemed the prettier of the two girls. In comparison, Emily looked rather like a gypsy. Thick dark hair, high cheekbones, large dark eyes, and a full lower lip combined to give her an exotic look in stark contrast to her sister's proper English Miss. Emily's unconventional looks were the despair of her mother, who considered anything out of the common way to be, well, common. In her opinion, Emily looked more like a lusty farmer's daughter than the proper daughter of a baronet. It caused Lady Smithfield to question whether Sir John's ancestors were all they should be. (Of the superior quality of her own lineage she was never in doubt.) However, Lydia looked remarkably like she herself did at that age. So Lady Smithfield had centered all her hopes on Lydia. Emily could marry where she willed, as long as she married a respectable gentleman, but it was sweet, dutiful, gentle Lydia who her mother always felt sure would bring home the matrimonial prize.

"Whom should I tell first?" Lady Smithfield asked, her triumphant tone jolting her daughters out of their shocked contemplation of her announcement. "I shall write a letter this very moment to Cousin Harriet. Then there's Sir John's side of the family—"

"Mama," Lydia interrupted, her voice slightly higher-pitched than usual. "Mama," she repeated, a little more calmly, "before we tell anyone, could we please keep the news to ourselves for a bit longer? After all, we've not heard from Lord Wesleigh as of yet. We have no knowledge of his agreement to his father's plan."

"My dear child, the duke is a man of honor. He would not raise our hopes only to dash them to the ground. You may rest assured that his word is as good as carved in stone."

Lydia did not appear comforted by this piece of information. Quite the opposite, in fact. Emily, who was unused to seeing her sister's calm composure disturbed, interceded in her behalf. "I think what Lydia means to say is that she needs time to accustom herself to the idea of being affianced. After all, the betrothal is not to be published for thirty days."

Lady Smithfield considered Emily's suggestion for a moment while both girls waited. "Perhaps you are right, Emily," she finally replied, and Lydia relaxed visibly. "We shall wait until Lord Wesleigh comes for a visit. That will be the appropriate time to make the announcement. I shall write his father immediately to inquire when Lord Wesleigh is to arrive. I am a little surprised His Grace did not mention it in his letter. No matter, I am sure he intends to come soon. In the meantime, we had better start planning your trousseau, Lydia. We shall most likely have to make a trip up to London. We cannot trust the dressmakers here in Stonehurst, or even in Hastings, to make a wardrobe worthy of a duchess."

Leaving their mother happily making wedding plans, the girls slipped upstairs. Once in the safety of her bedchamber, Lydia's beautiful blue eyes filled with tears. "Oh, Emily, what am I to do?"

"I take it you're not pleased with the notion of becoming Lady Wesleigh."

"Why *would* I be pleased? I do not even know the gentleman!"

"No, you do not know him. But who is to say he is not the epitome of charm and masculine beauty? We do know that he is young. The duchess was only a year or two older than Mama, so her son could not be more than thirty. You should be grateful they are not trying to marry you off to some gouty, doddering old man. I know it is quite difficult, Lydia, but you should at least try to suspend judgment until you have actually met him."

"But I do not *love* him," Lydia said, her voice a mere whisper, her eyes downcast.

"Well," Emily replied in a bracing tone, "perhaps you will learn to love him. It is not as if you are in love with anyone else."

Lydia's quiet crying ended with a hiccough, and she turned abruptly to walk to the window. Emily looked suspiciously at her sister, who was avoiding eye contact with her. "Lydia? You are not in love with someone, are you? Lydia?"

"Of course not. With whom would I be in love?" she replied, fiddling nervously with the cornflower blue ribbon on her bodice.

"I have no idea. There are no eligible gentlemen in Stonehurst under the age of sixty. Except, of course, for—" She halted abruptly as Lydia looked up nervously. "Lydia, don't tell me you are in love with Jonathan Sedgewick! He is as poor as—as a chimney sweep! Mama would never allow it. He is a *vicar.*"

"Vicars are perfectly respectable."

"Respectable, yes. Rich, no. But I suppose that does not matter if you truly care for him. Do you?" Lydia nodded. "Then of course you must not marry Lord Wesleigh," Emily said.

"But, Emily, Mama is counting on me to marry a fortune. How could I disappoint her so?" It was obvious the notion of disappointing their mother was abhorrent to Lydia. Emily reflected wryly to herself that it was a good thing she did not suffer from a similar anxiety.

"You know what Mama is like," Emily told her sister. "She acts as though we are living in penury now that we are no longer at Rollings. It is absolute nonsense. We are perfectly comfortable here." Emily paused, a contemplative look on her face. "But there is a way we could avoid disappointing Mama without sacrificing you at the marriage altar." Emily thought for a moment, while Lydia watched her in anticipation. "Yes, I think it would serve very well," Emily said slowly.

"What is it?" Lydia asked.

"I could marry Lord Wesleigh in your stead."

This calm announcement was met with a moment of shocked silence, before Lydia instinctively protested. "Oh, no, Emily, I cannot let you," she stated, shaking her head.

"Lydia, be reasonable. I am very unlikely to meet any prospective husbands here in Stonehurst now that my sister has chosen the only eligible man in the vicinity. I have to marry one day, and I am not the beauty you are. And just think of poor Lord Wesleigh," Emily said, struggling to keep a straight face but unable to contain a mischievous smile. "We cannot just let an eligible young marquess wither on the vine."

Lydia did not smile at Emily's droll remark, but only regarded her in silence. Emily shrugged, growing more serious. "And as you said, we do not want to disappoint Mama," she added.

"But Emily, it is such a sacrifice," Lydia protested.

The gleam returned to Emily's dark eyes, and she grinned impishly. "A sacrifice? To marry a wealthy young lord and live the pampered life of a duchess? I do not think most young ladies would view it as such. I will marry him if he is not despicable and he will have me. But from what we know of him, he does not appear to be particular. He agreed to marry you, and you are not even acquainted."

இ⊙෬

Alexander Eaton, Marquess of Wesleigh, and heir to the dukedom of Alford, was totally unaware that a trio of females he had yet to meet had decided his future. In fact, he was blissfully unaware of anything at all, being sound asleep after having arrived home in the wee hours of the morning. So he was none too pleased to hear a knock at his door, followed by the sound of someone entering his chamber.

"My lord, you've received an urgent summons from your father."

"Somebody die?" Wesleigh muttered thickly.

"Excuse me, my lord?"

"Did someone die?" Wesleigh repeated in a louder voice, albeit only a trifle more distinguishable, as it was muffled by the pillow he had pulled over his head.

"I should hope not, my lord, but I would not know."

"Well, in that case, Jenkins, I expect I had best find out what this is about."

"I should think so, my lord."

Wesleigh sighed and rolled over in bed. If only Jenkins weren't so dashed good with a cravat, he'd replace him with a valet who possessed a sense of humor. "And a face that would not curdle cream," he muttered to himself, ignoring Jenkins's look of inquiry.

As he dressed, he wondered what was behind his father's summons. It was not like the old man to issue commands like that. Besides the occasional supper together at Alford House, his father usually left him to his own devices. He hoped this wasn't about the aborted duel he'd taken part in the previous week. Both men had been foxed when the challenge was made, and when they sobered up the next morning, they realized they had made a mistake and deloped. Surely his father wouldn't summon him about something so insignificant as that.

Or could it be he'd taken offense at Alexander's latest entry in White's betting book? It had indeed been in poor taste to place a wager on the number of weeks after Lord Montville's recent demise that his young widow would remarry, but it was only a harmless jest. A bit childish, perhaps, but surely not so heinous a crime as to precipitate an urgent meeting.

So it was in a state of mingled anticipation, curiosity, and trepidation that Alexander finally entered Alford House and his father's study. The duke looked up as his son entered, and it seemed to Alexander that his father had aged a few years in the fortnight or so since he'd last seen him. Stanley Eaton, duke of Alford, presented an imposing appearance to some, being a large man with a prominent nose and big, bushy eyebrows. But the sharp, alert expression Alexander was accustomed to was missing this morning. Alexander hadn't seen his father look so weary since his mother's death.

"You wished to see me, Father?"

"Yes, Alexander. Please sit down." The older man waited for his son to take a seat before continuing. "I summoned you, Alexander, to discuss your future."

"My future?" Alexander repeated, somewhat surprised. This was not at all what he had expected, but he was a bit relieved that his past was not going to be the topic of discussion.

"Yes. Your future. Have you given it any thought?"

Alexander barely considered the question. "No more than the next chap, I suppose."

"I did not think so. Alexander, you are nearing thirty. Did you think you could continue on in this manner forever? Engaging men in duels for sport and making short shrift of a lady's reputation?"

Alexander flushed and sat up straighter in his chair. Apparently his past was on the agenda. "I wondered if you had heard about those incidents."

"They merely top your already illustrious career." The duke sighed, rubbing his forehead wearily. "I believe you to be an intelligent, responsible young man at heart, Alexander, but you are frittering your life away. And I cannot stand by and do nothing any longer."

"What do you mean to do?"

"I have already done it. I have written to a lady who was a close friend of your mother's, a Lady Elizabeth Smithfield. Your mother and she had fond hopes that you would one day marry Lady Smithfield's daughter Lydia. Well, the day has come. I proposed that in thirty days, unless she had an objection, the notice of her daughter's betrothal to my son would appear in the *Morning Post*. Lady Smithfield probably received the letter this very morning."

Alexander was momentarily speechless. The gall of his father's action infuriated him. He was not a child, however childishly he had behaved in the past, and he would not be dictated to. "I am very appreciative of the honor you do me, sir, but I am afraid I must refuse your very flattering proposal," he said through clenched jaws.

"Do not be sarcastic with me, young man. You know

I cannot go back on my word."

Alexander felt himself losing his fragile hold on his temper. "I cannot understand why you made such a suggestion in the first place. You cannot have expected me to submit quietly to an arranged marriage with a woman I have never met. The idea is preposterous. It's . . . it's medieval," he sputtered, running a hand through his dark hair and disarranging his careful toilette.

"I understand your anger, Alexander, and I dislike putting you in such a predicament." Alexander looked up, hopeful that his father could still be persuaded to change his mind, only to be disappointed as his father continued implacably. "But you have been on the town now for nearly a decade and have shown no inclination to make your own choice. The few women you do consort with are totally unfit to become the next duchess of Alford."

"I hope you at least trust me to know the difference between a lady of quality and a light-skirt!" Alexander shot back, standing up abruptly and beginning to pace about the room. His father's words wounded him deeply, but he was pained even further by the knowledge that it was his own behavior that had caused his father to form such a poor opinion of him.

The duke was moved by his son's obvious distress. "I am not an ogre, Alexander. I will not force you to marry a young lady you could not esteem. If you and the girl cannot come to an agreement, I will forgo making an announcement. But," he added, as a dazed smile of relief lit Alexander's face, "do not think that means you are relieved of all responsibility. If I do not find that you have made every effort to make yourself agreeable to

Miss Smithfield in the next thirty days, then I will be forced to cut off your allowance. You'll find that your free and easy lifestyle is not so easy to maintain on an empty purse."

Alexander nodded his agreement to his father's terms. He realized it was time he settled down, so if he liked the girl well enough, he supposed he might as well marry her. And if he did not, well, his father had loosened the noose around his neck just enough that he might be able to slip through.

"If you are concerned about Miss Smithfield's appearance, you needn't be. I would not expect you to marry a woman you found unattractive. I made her acquaintance four years ago at a wedding. She was only seventeen at the time, but already blossoming into a beautiful young lady with a pleasing demeanor. She is tall and slender, with light brown hair and fine blue eyes."

To Alexander, she sounded just like every other milk-and-water miss he had ever met at Almack's. "Why is it such a vision of pulchritude is still single at the ripe old age of twenty-one?" He asked, half-jokingly.

"Miss Smithfield was to have a London season her eighteenth year, but it was cut short when her father fell ill. She and her mother returned home immediately, and a month or two later Sir John passed away. The estate was entailed on a distant cousin, and Lady Smithfield and her daughters were forced to relocate. They now reside in the village of Stonehurst, where they have been the past two years or more. I assume they no longer have the finances to expend on a London season. Sir John left them comfortably enough, from what I have heard, but the cost of another residence probably took a large portion of their settlement."

Alexander was dismayed by his father's story. If the Smithfields were financially depressed, his father's offer would seem like their salvation. What self-respecting mother would not jump at the chance to marry her daughter to the heir of a wealthy duke? He could behave like an ill-mannered boor and they would pronounce him charming. He tugged uncomfortably at his exquisite cravat, which Jenkins must have tied too tightly that morning, for it suddenly felt as if it were choking him.

Two

ಶುಞ

Stonehurst. Stonehurst. As Lord Wesleigh left Alford House to walk the short distance to his own residence, he struggled to recall why that name sounded so
familiar. He knew he had heard it before, in a completely
different context. He was walking up the steps of his
town house when he finally remembered.

"Of course," he said aloud, "Sedgewick!"

The butler, who had just opened the door to let his
master in, wondered at Lord Wesleigh's sudden bout of
forgetfulness after his nearly ten years of service. Shaking
his head at the vagaries of the nobility, he nevertheless
reminded him, "Simmons, my lord."

"What is that, Simmons?" asked Wesleigh, startled
from his reverie. "Oh, you thought I was referring to
you. No, I was referring to my good friend, Jonathan
Sedgewick, the vicar in Stonehurst. I intend to pay him a
visit. Jenkins," he hollered, taking the stairs that led to
his second-story bedchamber two at a time, "pack our
bags. We are going to Stonehurst."

An hour later, as Wesleigh stood surveying the
mountain of luggage that his finicky valet considered
essential for a short visit to the country, he realized that
it would not do. It would not do at all. The half-
formulated plan he had been thinking through since he'd

realized he had a connection in Stonehurst was contingent on his ability to arrive virtually unnoticed on the village scene, not to arrive in ducal splendor with his crested carriage and a small army of servants.

He had what he felt was a perfectly normal desire to observe what his future held before being presented with it on a silver platter. If Lydia Smithfield had any major defects of personality or character, she would take the greatest care to hide these from her prospective bridegroom, the heir to a dukedom. Therefore, he intended to pose as someone so insignificant, so far beneath her notice, that she would be at no pains to hide her true self from him.

He thought first about masquerading as a servant, but quickly changed his mind. He preferred to at least pose as a member of the gentry, albeit a lesser member. Besides, he doubted his ability to play the part of a servant convincingly enough, particularly for any length of time. There had to be some sort of position he could occupy in Sedgewick's household, some minor, but realistic, role he could perform that would not cause undue notice.

He could not say what finally caused him to stumble upon the notion of posing as a curate, but it seemed a realistic enough disguise. No one would question a curate coming to visit his close friend, the vicar. And a curate was low enough on the social ladder that his entrance into Stonehurst society would cause barely a ripple. That is, if he traveled, dressed, and acted as a curate would. Which meant leaving Jenkins and his freshly laundered cravats behind.

"I have changed my mind, Jenkins. I will pack a small

bag myself. And you are to remain here in London."

Wesleigh had the satisfaction of seeing his valet's perpetually expressionless face assume a look of dismay. "But, my lord—"

"I shall be taking the stage to Stonehurst, and I doubt there would be room for the other passengers were I to take such an impressive array of baggage."

"The stage, my lord? Do I understand you properly? You cannot mean that you, the heir to the duke of Alford, are taking the common stage from London to Stonehurst."

"Yes, that is exactly what I mean. And I need you to see about securing my passage. I would prefer the box-seat, but any outside seat will do, I suppose. It would be criminal to have to be shut inside on a day like today." Wesleigh turned to search for his plainest jacket, preferably one a few seasons old as well, before realizing that his valet still stood rooted in place, his mouth hanging open. "Jenkins, I haven't a lot of time to spare. I am hoping to make Stonehurst by nightfall." Turning back to his wardrobe, he pulled out an old, badly cut jacket he'd never worn. "Ah, this should do nicely," he said to himself. As he removed the jacket he was wearing, a sartorial masterpiece of Weston's, Jenkins shuddered violently, and left to do his master's bidding.

৪০০৪

The Smithfield ladies and, indeed, every inhabitant of Smithfield House, were on pins and needles awaiting the arrival of Lord Wesleigh. Even though Lady Smithfield had stuck to her promise of keeping silent about the match, the servants, who invariably came to know of any circumstance in their mistresses' lives, had somehow succeeded in ferreting out this secret as well.

Emily was perhaps more anxious than anyone for the marquess to arrive, although her mother ran a close second. Lady Smithfield was terribly frustrated to have to keep the secret of her daughter's conquest. She was desperate to tell her closest friends, not to mention her greatest enemies. Lydia was anxious, also, but not for the marquess to arrive. For the first time in her life, the kindhearted young lady was wishing an accident to befall someone. Not anything serious, mind, just serious enough to lay him up for a few weeks and somehow prevent him from marrying her or her sister. Because no matter what Emily said, Lydia could not believe that her dear sister could really wish to sacrifice herself in such a manner.

Emily assured her sister repeatedly that it was no sacrifice. If anything, she was fearful that her mother and the duke would not accept her as a substitute for Lydia. She was determined to ensure her sister's romance with the vicar came to fruition, or she feared that Lydia would be forced to marry Wesleigh no matter what she wished. Or what Emily wished.

For Emily dearly wanted to marry the marquess. She had moments of doubt, when her stubborn little heart yearned for something like Lydia had found. Someone who loved her and wanted *her*, not because his father ordered him to, but because his heart did. But then she would sternly push those thoughts aside. *Be sensible, Emily,* she told herself. *How would you ever meet such a man in Stonehurst?* And then, once again, she would look forward eagerly to the marquess's arrival.

It was not that Emily was materialistic or grasping, determined to be a duchess at all costs. It was just that she was *bored!* She was incredibly bored, there in dull, poky little Stonehurst. She wanted to go to balls and masquerades, attend the opera and the theater, and meet people, famous people, like Lord Byron, and the Prince Regent. She wanted to travel to the Continent, to faraway, only-dreamed-of places like Venice and Rome. She would look longingly at pictures of elegant ensembles in *La Belle Assemblée*, only to look despairingly in the mirror at the missish dress that the village dressmaker churned out. Lydia, on the other hand, cared nothing for any of these things. When quizzed about her aborted season in London, she could only say that she did not care for London, finding it very dirty and crowded. She would be perfectly content to stay in Stonehurst forever. Life was so unfair!

But Emily was determined that, with a little resourcefulness and ingenuity, she could change her fate. And, instead of sitting and twiddling her thumbs until the marquess arrived, she could start by sealing her sister's fate. And the vicar's.

§∞Q

The time for Sunday services finally arrived, to the satisfaction of many, for various reasons, and none of them spiritually motivated. Emily was anxious to begin her plan of aiding Lydia and the vicar in their romance, Lydia was anxious to catch even a sight of her beloved, and the vicar was not loath to see Lydia, either. But perhaps the person with the greatest interest in attending the services was a visitor to Stonehurst, Lord Wesleigh.

Of course, for the purpose of his visit he was not to be known as Lord Wesleigh, but rather, Alexander Williams. This had much distressed his friend Jonathan Sedgewick, when Alexander had revealed his plan to him a few days earlier.

"You wish to pose as a curate? But why?" Sedgewick had asked, after the initial greetings had been exchanged. Jonathan Sedgewick was a handsome young man, with fair hair and blue eyes. Alexander had always liked Sedgewick, but there was no denying he took himself a little too seriously. Alexander should have known Sedgewick would not react well to the little masquerade he had planned.

"That is a long story, my friend, and one that does me little credit," Alexander replied, still stinging from his father's words earlier that day.

"I would like to hear it, just the same."

So Alexander explained that his father thought it time he was married, and had arranged a match for him with a Miss Smithfield, whom he had never even laid eyes on.

"Miss Smithfield!" Sedgewick exclaimed loudly.

"Yes," Alexander said, a little startled by the vehemence of his friend's response. "Miss Smithfield. Her mother went to some ladies' academy with my mother. Apparently they have nothing better to do at those schools than sit around and discuss the futures of their unborn offspring."

Sedgewick did not respond to his friend's attempt at humor. He still appeared to be in a state of shock. "But it cannot be, not Miss *Lydia* Smithfield. Could it have possibly been Miss Emily Smithfield?" he asked.

"I think I would recall the name of the lady, if nothing else. She is the eldest of the Smithfield daughters."

"Yes, Lydia is the eldest." The thought seemed to depress Sedgewick greatly, and he became silent and distracted. Alexander stared at him quizzically, wondering what had come over his friend, but having his suspicions. "There is nothing wrong with the lady, I trust?"

"Of course not!" Sedgewick answered, his eyes taking on a faraway look. "A more beautiful, caring, wonderful girl does not exist in the entire world!"

"That is quite a testimonial. I suppose, then, I should thank my father for engaging me to her." As Sedgewick seemed, if possible, to grow more depressed at this statement, Alexander smiled to himself. It seemed that this charade might not even be necessary. That is, if the young lady returned his friend's obvious regard. But, even if she did, it was unlikely that her family would countenance her match with a vicar. No, he had better proceed with his plan. "But," Alexander continued, "I cannot be thankful to my father for his high-handed manner of securing me a wife. So that is why I intend to pose as a curate. It will give me time to observe the lady and decide if I think we should suit. My father did make a stipulation that if we could not, he would not force the match."

Sedgewick was not cheered by this bit of news. Knowing Lydia as he did, he was sure the marquess would take one look and fall head over heels in love with her. Yet he reluctantly agreed to make the introduction Sunday after the service was over. He also agreed to let Alexander borrow some of his jackets, even when Alexander inadvertently insulted him by saying it was because he did not want to present too fine an appearance.

Throughout the sermon, Alexander steeled himself to face his fate. He did not hear one word of the service, but from the abstracted manner of Sedgewick's delivery, it was clear he had not missed much. Alexander did not know if he were more worried that he would like Lydia or dislike her. If he did like her, there was now the added complication of his friend Sedgewick's evident regard for her. If he did not like her, he would disappoint his father and her entire family.

Alexander had yet to see the Smithfield ladies, as he was seated at the front of the church. When the service ended, he glanced casually around, and, as it was a small parish, with very few young ladies, he picked out a trio of ladies he felt could be the Smithfields. But, as they were headed out into the churchyard, he saw little other than the backs of their bonnets.

He waited for Sedgewick, and they proceeded into the open air. With their similar expressions of heroic resignation, they more closely resembled soldiers going to battle than eligible young men about to meet nubile young ladies.

Alexander had to wait a moment for his eyes to ad-just to the afternoon sun after entering the churchyard. Then he looked around for the ladies he had glimpsed earlier. "Is that her?" he asked Sedgewick under his breath, nodding toward a group of females.

Sedgewick followed his friend's line of vision and nodded. Miss Smithfield turned and faced Alexander directly, and he looked her over carefully, before breath-ing a sigh of relief. His father had not been exaggerating when he had stated she was beautiful. But she did not quite match his father's description. "I thought my father described her as being fairer," he told Sedgewick.

Sedgewick shrugged. "She is not blond, but I would not describe her as dark-haired, either."

"What are you talking about? Of course she has—" Alexander broke off abruptly, as he noticed another young lady standing next to what he was already thinking of as *his* young lady. And this lady had lighter hair and blue eyes. Apparently the first lady he had seen was the younger sister. He could hardly contain his disappointment as Sedgewick led him forward to make the introductions. But, then again, what was he thinking? He had no wish to be leg-shackled, not to either of the Smithfield daughters.

Emily had noticed the gentleman with the vicar and was quite intrigued. She had never seen anyone so handsome. She knew many considered Jonathan Sedgewick to be attractive, but she much preferred this gentleman, with his dark hair and intense brown eyes. She was a little embarrassed, however, by the thorough perusal she had just received from him. She studied him covertly, while the introductions were made, and was shocked to discover he was a curate. He carried himself as if he were a lord! No curate she ever knew would have looked at a lady the way he had just looked at her. He looked her way again, and she lowered her eyes in confusion, embarrassed to have been caught gawking at him like a schoolgirl. When she finally raised her eyes, she was miffed to see that he was studying Lydia as intently as he had her. *Foolish girl,* she chided herself, *why would you want the attention of a curate, anyway?*

She listened intently as her mother spoke to the gentlemen, too nervous to add anything to the conversation, her eyes straying far too often to Mr. Williams's perfect features. So intent was she with trying to sort out these new, inexplicable sensations, she completely forgot her resolve to involve Lydia and Sedgewick together in conversation, and they stood as mute as she, while her mother invited the curate to dinner that evening. The dinner party was the first maneuver in Emily's plan to get Lydia and Jonathan Sedgewick together. She had convinced her mother that they needed to entertain some of the local families in the parish, to repay them for the many kindnesses they had received since they had moved to the area just over two years ago. The vicar was on the guest list, and now it seemed that his friend, Mr. Williams, was as well. Emily felt her plans were proceeding well. But she didn't know yet how Mr. Williams fit into them.

Three

ഐ

Dinner was a dull affair, as Emily was seated far from Mr. Williams, who was the only person of interest at the table. Emily assured herself she felt that way because he was new in town, and she had known all the others at the table for more than two years. Regardless, she found her eyes straying to the other end of the table more often than was proper, and she quickly lowered her eyes and looked away when she caught him looking at her as well. *Stop making a fool of yourself, Emily, just because he's the handsomest man you've ever seen,* she told herself. *There are probably scores of gentlemen like him in London.*

Mr. Thistle, the local magistrate, was seated to Emily's left. He was a bachelor but, being over sixty, was not an object of much interest to the young ladies. Even so, Emily usually honored him with a light flirtation, as he had an eye for a pretty girl, and she knew he enjoyed teasing her. Tonight, however, she paid Mr. Thistle little heed, her thoughts distracted by Mr. Williams, until she heard Mr. Thistle mention the highwayman.

"What highwayman?" she asked, her first contribution to the conversation other than a polite nod here and there.

The old man was delighted to have Emily's attention.

"You must have heard talk of it by now."

Emily assured him she had not.

"Ah. What a novel position for me to enjoy. It is unusual that I, a gentleman, am able to import some small bit of news to a lady. " Mr. Thistle chuckled at his own witticism, until Emily reminded him that he had not yet shared his bit of news.

"Yes. Well it seems some brigand has robbed three carriages, on the London road, only a few miles outside Stonehurst."

"How shocking," Emily replied, her interest truly caught. "I hope no one has been injured?"

"Not yet; apparently there has not been cause. In each case, the inhabitants of the carriage surrendered their belongings without protest. I happen to believe that the wise course. Of what value is some trinket in comparison with one's life?" Emily murmured her agreement. "If you ladies make a trip to town, or even to Rye or Hastings, be very careful."

Emily agreed that they would, and before she had a chance to ask any other questions, her mother was giving the signal that it was time to leave the gentlemen to their port, and the ladies retired to the drawing room, where the talk was all of the mysterious highwayman.

"I have heard that he is very gallant, and there is even talk of him being a gentleman fallen onto hard circumstances," one of the ladies offered.

"Nonsense." Lady Abernathy contradicted in a voice that would brook no argument. "He's a common thief. No gentleman of my acquaintance would ever behave in such a dastardly fashion." Lady Abernathy was the wife of an earl, and took her position very seriously. She had steel gray curls that looked as though they were hard to the touch, as did all of her tall, skinny, angular body. Her posture seemed almost painfully straight, as if she had a poker down the back of her dress. It made Emily dreadfully aware of her own posture, and she always strained to sit straighter when Lady Abernathy was present.

Since no one dared contradict Lady Abernathy, who outranked everyone in the room, it was probably a good thing the gentlemen chose to rejoin the ladies soon after her pronouncement. Lady Smithfield promptly suggested Lydia entertain the guests by playing the pianoforte for them.

"I have a much better notion, Mama," Emily announced. "You know that while Lydia plays divinely, she has an even prettier singing voice. And I believe I have noticed the vicar's pleasing baritone at church, as well. Why don't I play the pianoforte, and Lydia and Mr. Sedgewick can favor us with a duet."

Lydia and Sedgewick looked less than pleased at this idea, and Lady Smithfield looked none too happy either, but Lord Abernathy took up the idea wholeheartedly, mentioning he loved to hear a duet.

Satisfied her plan was working, Emily consulted with the two reluctant singers on a selection. They all agreed to a simple ballad, and Emily began to play. She was sorry that her position at the instrument didn't enable her to see their expressions, but they sounded romantic enough, and at least it should start them thinking, singing a love song together. She did manage to sneak one peek behind her, and was unhappy to see Mr. Williams studying the two as intently as she was.

Everyone clapped loudly at the conclusion of the song, and before Emily could suggest another duet, Lady Smithfield hurried to remind Lydia that it was her turn to play for them. Emily graciously retired and sought a seat next to the vicar.

"I hope you didn't mind my suggestion that you and Lydia should sing. I thought you both performed wonderfully."

"Well, I would have preferred not to have been thrust into the center of things as I was, but I must admit it was rather enjoyable."

"I felt it would have been a shame if you and Lydia never had the chance to sing together. I think you are a perfect match." As Jonathan colored at this and looked rather alarmed, Emily thought she had gone a little too far and amended her statement. "Your voices, I mean. They seem perfectly matched."

Jonathan thanked her rather huffily and excused himself, and Emily realized she'd have a hard time getting these two together, blessed, as they both were, with a surfeit of propriety.

"Are you trying your hand at a little matchmaking, Miss Smithfield?"

Emily jumped, as she hadn't seen Mr. Williams approach. Still, although her heart fluttered, she managed to answer composedly enough. "Was I that obvious?"

"Well, you were a trifle heavy-handed, but for a first attempt it was probably not so bad. At least, I assume it's your first attempt. You do not fit my notion of an experienced matchmaker."

"And just what is your notion of an experienced matchmaker?" Emily asked him, smiling up at him as he took the seat next to her.

A picture of his father rose briefly in his mind, and he smiled grimly to himself. "Oh, I don't know, older perhaps. Not quite so beautiful." He watched in wonder as Emily blushed and looked uncomfortable at this remark. He reminded himself that this was a country girl, unused to the attentions of gentlemen. For some reason that thought pleased him. As Emily had not responded to his compliment, he spoke again in an attempt to put her at ease. "I have no experience as a matchmaker myself, but it seems as though it would be a difficult endeavor."

"It is," Emily agreed, happy to have someone sympathize with her and even happier for the change of subject. "Especially when I have two such difficult subjects."

"May I ask why you persist, then, since it's obvious they're so unwilling to cooperate?"

"Oh, they are not unwilling, I assure you. At least," Emily amended, as she realized it was disloyal of her to betray her sister's confidence, "I do not believe them to be."

"And why is that?" Alexander was very interested in her answer, as he hoped it matched his own conclusions.

"Oh, it is just something you can tell. It is hard to describe. I suppose you'd have to be a lady to understand."

"Oh, I don't think so. I think gentlemen can sense these things as well."

Emily wondered if it was just her imagination that caused her to believe that they were no longer speaking just of Lydia and Mr. Sedgewick. She could not think of a thing to say in reply, and realized she and Mr. Williams were staring intently at each other. With an effort, she lowered her gaze.

"How long a visit do you make here, Mr. Williams?"

"I am not certain. There are extenuating circumstances." Alexander realized this was a strange reply and hurried to explain. "That is, I don't have a position at the moment, as I was serving in a parish on a temporary basis, until a vicar took over the living. Once he did, I was forced to look elsewhere, so I'm here staying with Sedgewick until another opportunity presents itself."

Emily was a little disappointed at his lack of ambition. He seemed intelligent and gentlemanly; in her opinion he could go farther than being a humble curate. But it occurred to her that she did not know him well enough to say so, and she held her tongue. She decided to try instead to convince him to aid her in her match-making schemes. As the vicar's close friend, he could influence him greatly. Before she could begin, Lady Smithfield interrupted.

"Emily, Lydia, Lady Abernathy proposes to have a ball."

"Truly?" Emily jumped up excitedly, while Lydia just smiled her acceptance of the treat. "What is the occasion?"

"Oh, none in particular, although we'll probably invite some young men down from London. It's high time someone showed an interest in you girls, before you're left on the shelf completely." Lady Abernathy chuckled somewhat mechanically, to show it was just a joke, while Lady Smithfield bristled.

"It just so happens, Lady Abernathy, that Lydia's received—"

"Mama," Emily interrupted, while Lydia could only look on, terrified. "It was to be our little secret, but now that you've begun, I suppose we dare not leave our friends in suspense. Mama's referring to our new dressmaker, from whom Lydia commissioned a dress and has just received it. Now she'll be able to wear it to your ball."

"A new dressmaker. Here in Stonehurst?"

"No, no, I have already said too much, you shall just have to wait until your ball to hear the rest. Lydia would not want all the young ladies from miles around copying her dress."

Lady Abernathy looked satisfied, while Lady Smithfield was forced to swallow the news of Lydia's engagement once again. But she looked forward with pleasure to crowing about it to Lady Abernathy as soon as Lord Wesleigh arrived from London. If he ever did arrive.

The Abernathys were the highest ranking of the nobility in the parish, with the largest estate, Rothergate. They had one son, Viscount Farnwright, who would be attending the ball although he had already married and spent most of his time in London. Alexander was slightly acquainted with Farnwright, and was grateful that as a lowly curate no one would care whether he attended the ball or not. He noticed Emily's delight at the prospect of the ball and smiled to himself. She was a taking little thing. He hoped that she would make it to London one day for a season of her own. It was too bad his mother was not still living or she might have offered to take the girl under her wing. He dismissed that thought and pondered instead the little scene he had just witnessed. It seemed as though Lady Smithfield had been about to announce the news of Lydia's engagement before Emily interrupted. He was thankful, of course, as he had no desire to publicize the betrothal, but he wondered that the Smithfield family didn't shout it from the rooftops. It would be to Emily's advantage if her sister married well. It would put her in the way of meeting eligible gentleman. But, from her behavior earlier that evening, it was obvious she had different plans in mind for her sister. Just what was the little minx up to?

He noticed all of a sudden that Lord Abernathy was staring at him, and he racked his brain to think of any way he could have drawn attention to himself.

"Where's your living?" Lord Abernathy asked.

"I am sorry, my lord, I don't have one at the moment. In between positions, you might say."

"I know of one in the next county over that's vacant. Should talk to Lord Billingsworth about it."

"Thank you, my lord, I'll consider it." There was no way Alexander would speak to Billingsworth. He and Billingsworth, while not intimates, both belonged to the same club, and Billingsworth would be sure to recognize him.

"What's there to consider, young man? Positions don't grow on trees. You should jump at the opportunity." Lord Abernathy was looking at him strangely, and Alexander realized a penniless young curate with no living would not have dismissed his offer so cavalierly.

"You are right, my lord, of course. I will be sure to look into it at the earliest opportunity."

Abernathy nodded in satisfaction, and Alexander mentally chided himself for slipping out of his role so easily. It was a good thing he hadn't posed as a servant.

Apparently he had no talent for acting. He needed to
accomplish his goal, so that he could return to London
as soon as possible and quit this stupid charade. His father would certainly never expect him to pursue a lady
whose affections were already engaged by another. He
just needed to verify his suspicions and present his father
with the evidence. Miss Emily Smithfield would be the
perfect accomplice in his endeavor. Not to mention a
most attractive one.

ଈଓଙ

Emily was at that moment peering speculatively
across the room at Alexander, thinking much along those
same lines herself. She was very conscious of the fact that
Lord Wesleigh could appear any day, and there was still
nothing resolved between Lydia and Sedgewick. If he
were to arrive tomorrow, Emily doubted she could do
anything to prevent the match from proceeding as
planned. And in addition to her own selfish reasons for
wishing to stop her sister's marriage, she truly loved her
sister and did not want her marrying one man when she
loved another. But Emily was accomplishing nothing on
her own. She needed Mr. Williams's help. He was
Sedgewick's good friend and could ascertain if Sedgewick returned Lydia's regard. He had told her earlier that
evening he had no experience with matchmaking, but
Emily was sure he was a quick learner. He didn't seem
the sort who was unfamiliar with romance. She would
wager he'd been an eager participant in quite a few *af-
faires de coeur.* Alexander saw Emily looking at him and
smiled. Emily caught her breath before smiling shyly
back. He got up to walk toward her, and Emily was held,

captivated by his stare. It was as if they were the only two people in the room. She jumped when Lady Abernathy turned to speak to her.

"I have another treat in store for you, young lady."

"Oh, really?" Emily replied absently, still watching Williams's progress across the room. "What is that?"

"I am having a visit from my niece, Lady Cynthia Sommers. You will want to meet her. She could definitely smarten you up." Emily wondered that Lady Abernathy dared to criticize her appearance, as Lady Abernathy was no nonpareil in that area, either. Her favorite color appeared to be a quite unbecoming mixture of brown and gray. "Quite the fashion plate, my niece," Lady Abernathy continued in her stentorian voice. "Has all the London bucks chasing after her. She could definitely teach you a thing or two, young lady."

Emily was embarrassed to have Lady Abernathy proclaim in front of Mr. Williams that she needed someone to help her attract beaux, but he hardly seemed to have heard. At the very mention of the name Lady Cynthia, a dismayed look appeared on his face, and he halted abruptly. He regained his composure almost immediately and took the seat next to Emily.

Alexander was quite perturbed, however, to hear that Lady Cynthia was coming to Stonehurst. They had enjoyed an enjoyable flirtation last season, until the lady had made it very clear she would not be averse to something more. He had spent the end of the season last year and the beginning of this one avoiding her. He assuredly had not expected to run into her in this little backwater. He assumed she would be enjoying the height of the season. Could she have heard somehow he was in Stonehurst? It was not an impossibility. He had sent his father a note before he left explaining that he was leaving for Stonehurst at the earliest opportunity to make Miss Smithfield's acquaintance. It was entirely conceivable that the news had spread. He would have to think later how he would deal with her presence, but, for now, Lady Abernathy had resumed conversation with Lady Smithfield, and this was his opportunity to speak to Emily.

"I found our earlier conversation very interesting, Miss Smithfield."

"As did I, Mr. Williams. I wished to discuss the matter with you further." Emily felt she might have been a trifle bold, but Mr. Williams just smiled.

"Good. For I must admit I had a similar goal in mind when I approached you. I feel that a gentleman such as my friend Sedgewick, a gentleman with such serious responsibilities, could only benefit by having a partner and helper. A proper wife can be the making of a man, don't you agree, Miss Smithfield?"

"I am in complete agreement. Your friend needs a compassionate and caring wife, who will assist him in his parish duties and provide a good example to others."

"I take it from your matchmaking attempt earlier this evening you feel that your sister meets those qualifications."

"Well, perhaps I should not say so to a near stranger, but I must admit they seem well suited."

"You can trust me, Miss Smithfield, for I have Sedgewick's best interests at heart. And somehow I feel that I know you very well, although our acquaintance has been of short duration. There is a candid, honest quality about you that is quite refreshing."

"Thank you for the compliment, Mr. Williams, but my mother is more forthright in her description of me. The quality you describe so prettily as 'candid and honest' she more accurately characterizes as 'a sad lack of delicacy.'"

"Then your mother does you an injustice. Please believe me when I tell you that I do not find you lacking."

Emily was so unused to compliments that she barely knew how to react. She decided it would be best just to change the subject, although she meant to hone her skills at flirtation before the marquess arrived. That thought reminded her of the goal at hand, which she had been in imminent danger of forgetting. Mr. Williams's gorgeous brown eyes were proving a formidable distraction. "As you appreciate candor, I will tell you truthfully that I wish to enlist your help in throwing Lydia and Mr. Sedgewick together. I was hoping you could also tell me if you have any reason to believe Mr. Sedgewick holds my sister in esteem."

Alexander wondered again why Emily was so determined for her sister to marry a vicar. He had his own reasons for wishing for the match, but why would Emily wish her sister to make such an inferior match from a worldly standpoint? Had she taken him in dislike before even meeting him? He found that notion displeased him for some reason, but then again, what did it matter if it left him free? Emily was still waiting for him to reply, and he felt it would do no harm to give her his true opinion.

"He has not confided in me, of course, but I could not help but notice he appears to admire her. I believe he would not be at all averse to a match if he believed it to be possible. I think that is his secret hope, but he feels she is above his touch, and so has tried to put the thought out of his mind." Emily nodded, delighted with this bit of news. She had felt much the same way herself, but was pleased to have it confirmed. "And your sister, Miss Smithfield? Do you have reason to believe she's partial to Mr. Sedgewick?"

"Yes, I do. That is why I'm determined to see them together." Emily looked at him, considering how much to confide in him. The look in his warm brown eyes must have convinced her, because she continued. "You see, there is another gentleman, with greater advantages from a material and social standpoint, whom my mother would prefer to see Lydia marry. But I do not think such things should be a consideration when two people truly love one another, do you?"

If asked that question even a day previously, Alexander would have laughed and scoffed at the idea of love being a prerequisite of marriage. In his social circle, men and women married to achieve greater social standing and wealth. He knew very few that married for love. But looking now at Emily, who was waiting innocently for a reply, he surprised himself with his answer. "I, too, feel that none of those considerations should matter when compared with the feelings of two people toward one another," he told her. He was rewarded by a bright smile from Emily, which made him feel guilty for holding such cynical views in the past.

Lady Smithfield, who had greater ambitions for Emily now that her sister was making so creditable a match, was displeased to see her paying such close attention to a penniless curate. What had she been thinking to invite him for dinner? He was much too attractive. She called Emily away on some fictitious errand, but before the evening was over, Emily and Alexander were able to arrange an "accidental" meeting the next day in the village, with Lydia and Sedgewick in tow.

Four

Over breakfast the next morning, Emily and Lydia were alarmed to hear their mother announce the arrival of another missive from the duke of Alford.

Lady Smithfield eagerly scanned the letter while her daughters silently waited. "How peculiar," Lady Smithfield finally said, her brow wrinkled in confusion. "The duke writes that Lord Wesleigh left London for Stonehurst Friday last week. Stonehurst is only a four-hour trip from London. He should have arrived by now. I hope he did not suffer an accident along the way."

Emily was relieved. Whatever was delaying Wesleigh she hoped it continued to delay him for at least another sennight. She needed more time to push Lydia's romance along. She doubted even a sennight would be long enough, but it was better than nothing.

Lydia was guilt-stricken. She was sure her hope that Wesleigh would meet with an accident had been fulfilled. How could she have been so evil as to wish bad on her fellowman? If Wesleigh arrived this instant, she would gladly marry him, if only as penance for the wicked thoughts she'd entertained toward him.

Lady Smithfield, who had continued to read the duke's letter, interrupted her daughters' tempestuous thoughts to make another announcement. "Oh, my. Oh, my! Lydia, Emily, the duke of Alford is coming here! He will arrive Tuesday evening next week. There is barely enough time to prepare! I must consult with Cook, and the Green Suite must be prepared, oh, heavens, there is so much to do. A duke, in my house. Who would have ever thought it? There is not a moment to lose." Lady Smithfield hurried from the dining room, while Lydia and Emily looked at each other in amazement.

Lydia broke the silence at last by announcing with a look of grim determination on her pretty face: "I think, Emily, that it's my duty to marry Lord Wesleigh."

"That is nonsense. Marriage should not be undertaken as a matter of *duty*. Just because you are too in awe of the duke to tell him that you do not wish to marry his son does not mean you should spend the rest of your life in misery. And not only you, but what of Sedgewick? And Wesleigh? They will both be miserable as well. Why, I'd say it's your duty *not* to go through with this sham of a marriage."

Lydia seemed much struck by this argument, as Emily hoped she would be. Her sister was a very obedient, dutiful girl, and it went against her nature to rebel against anything. But if Emily were to convince her a match with Sedgewick was the right thing to do, she might just be able to pull it off.

"Just think, Lydia, you will have to pledge before God that you will love, honor, and obey your husband. It would be a lie, feeling as you do about Sedgewick. You would not want to lie, would you Lydia?"

"I had not thought of it in that respect. You're right, Emily. That would be sinful. But if you married Lord Wesleigh, you would have to make the same vows. How could you do it?"

Emily had not expected to have her logic thrown back in her face. "If I were to make that vow, it would not be a lie, as I do not love any other gentleman, and I plan to do all in my power to make Lord Wesleigh a good wife," she finally managed to reply.

Lydia seemed satisfied with that response, but Emily continued to think about Lydia's question long after the conversation had ended. It was true that her heart did not belong to another, but she felt without very much effort she could lose it to Mr. Williams. He was so very attractive. When she spoke with him she felt an excitement that she had never known before. Could she marry a man who didn't make her pulse flutter like Mr. Williams did, whose eyes did not hold the sparkle and life that she saw in his? Then again, could she marry a man who did not even have a home to take her to, a penniless curate who seemed to be making little effort to advance? No. It was foolish to fall in love with such a man. Once Sedgewick's attachment to Lydia was assured, she would have no need to seek out Mr. Williams's company, and she would continue with her original plan of convincing Lord Wesleigh to have her as a wife, instead of Lydia.

Satisfied to have reached a proper conclusion to her dilemma, although unable to account for her sudden lowering of spirits, Emily sought out Lydia. It was time to convince her to walk with her to the village to buy some ribbons.

৪০৫

Emily had felt a pleasurable tinge of guilt the previous evening, making an assignation with Mr. Williams to meet him on the High Street in the morning, and she was experiencing a similar excitement at the prospect of seeing him again. She sternly told herself to stop being foolish, but she could barely school her features into an expression of calm disinterest when she saw him. Turning toward Lydia, she said as nonchalantly as she could manage: "Look there, Lydia. Mr. Sedgewick appears to be walking this way with his friend, Mr. Williams."

Lydia was having a hard time appearing disinterested herself. "I do believe you're right, Emily."

The girls acknowledged the gentlemen with a polite nod and a smile, which was all the encouragement the gentlemen needed to join them.

"If you ladies have finished all your errands, may we accompany you home?" Mr. Williams asked, falling into step with Emily.

"That would be lovely, thank you."

Emily and Williams trailed behind Lydia and Sedgewick, and Emily deliberately slowed her pace to put more distance between them.

"Twisted your ankle, have you?" Williams asked Emily, an expression of mock sympathy on his face.

"You know I have not; I am trying to allow Lydia and Sedgewick some time alone together," she hissed back at him, as Lydia and Sedgewick were still within hearing distance.

"You mustn't allow them to get too far ahead of us or she'll think she's been compromised."

"Why, that would be perfect, then they would have to marry."

"Yes, but is it part of your plan to put yourself in a compromising position with me?"

"No, of course not, that is the last thing in the world I want." Which wasn't entirely true, but it was what Emily had been trying to convince herself was true, so her denial may have been expressed a shade too vehemently.

Alexander was somewhat disappointed by this emphatic response, but then again, what did he expect? Had he expected her to announce that her fervent desire in life was to be forced to marry an undistinguished curate? What stunned him was how much he had wanted her to imply something of the sort. He swallowed his disappointment and decided instead to discover the answer to some of the questions that had been puzzling him.

"So if that is not your plan, then what is, if I may be so bold as to inquire?"

"Whatever do you mean? You know my plan. It is to see Lydia marry the man of her choice, the man she truly loves."

"This other man, the one you mentioned in our conversation the previous evening, is he so odious a man that Miss Smithfield cannot like him?" Alexander asked.

"Yes. No. Actually, I do not know. We have not made the gentleman's acquaintance."

"Yet you say he is Sedgewick's superior in position and fortune. Would not he be the better match for your sister?"

"No, he would not." Emily was frustrated by his question and answered a little irritably. "Aside from the fact that Lydia loves another, she would not be comfortable with life as a duchess. She much prefers a placid, bucolic sort of life, such as the life she enjoys here in Stonehurst."

"I take it from your tone of voice that you do not share your sister's tastes."

"No, I do not. While I admit the country is not without its charms, I find life here dull for the most part. I want something more than a country swain and a vicarage full of blue-eyed moppets. I am nineteen years old. I want to see a little of life before I settle into old age."

"I do not think you're in any danger of that for some time. Nineteen isn't such a great age, after all." Alexander replied, holding back a smile. "But we stray from the subject. Lydia has no ambition to be a duchess, but marrying her off to Sedgewick will not aid you in your schemes any. Unless you can convince this other gentleman to carry you off instead."

Emily's startled expression alerted him that he might have stumbled on to something. "That's your plan, isn't it, Miss Smithfield? To ensure Lydia's firmly out of the running for the gentleman's hand and offer yourself as the consolation prize."

Emily did not reply, but the look of embarrassment on her face was proof enough. Alexander was disgusted. So much for all her talk of marrying for love. She was just the countrified version of a Lady Cynthia. Perhaps worse. She was willing to cut her own sister out of the running. "I must say, I find all this a little hypocritical of you."

"Mr. Williams, you mustn't think badly of me. I truly have Lydia's best interests at heart." When Alexander did not reply, merely casting her a look of disgust, Emily hurried to explain. "You see, it is as I explained to you earlier, Lydia has no desire to be a duchess. Why, the very thought terrifies her. Then, when I discovered her attachment to Mr. Sedgewick, I was determined she should not have to make such a sacrifice."

"So you nobly offered to make the sacrifice in her stead."

"Well, yes, but, as you are implying, I did not see it as such a great sacrifice. I believe I would enjoy life in town, and I have not formed an attachment to another."

"As of yet. What happens when you meet a gentleman you could love, but you are already married to your precious lord."

"Well, I must say, the idea did not occur to me until just recently. I just assumed such a thing would not happen. Now I am not so sure."

Alexander was pleased to see she wasn't quite the heartless wench he'd thought her. Because if those big brown eyes staring up into his weren't sending the message that he was the one to have caused her doubts, his name wasn't Alexander Eaton, Marquess of Wesleigh. He chose to ignore that, for the moment, that was not his name.

"Your ambitions aside, you are correct that your sister should not be forced into a loveless marriage. Whether or not you should be the one to take her place is a concern for you and the duke, and has nothing to do with me." He smiled wryly as he made this statement, as it had everything to do with him. And then his sense of humor overtook him, and he had to restrain himself from laughing out loud. How ironic, he thought, that Emily was announcing her matrimonial plans to the very man she hoped to entrap.

Emily, who had been walking with downcast eyes, feeling ashamed, somehow, of what she had previously

felt was a logical and advantageous scheme for all involved, cast a tentative glance at Mr. Williams and was
surprised to see him grinning.

"I cannot possibly see what you find amusing in all
of this," Emily said, whose feelings of humility and
shame had vanished to be replaced with indignation.

"Can you not?" Mr. Williams asked, whose grin
widened when he saw the look of ferocity directed toward him, which put him in mind of a rather angry kit-
ten. "You don't find it somewhat amusing to consider
this young man—what is his name?"

"Lord Wesleigh."

"You don't find it the least bit amusing," Mr. Williams continued, "that Wesleigh, having already been
told to marry one girl, arrives on the scene and without
anybody asking his opinion, is told, 'Sorry old chap, that
one's been taken, but be a nice lad and marry this one
instead'?"

"Well, I do not see how it would matter to him. He
agreed to marry one girl he has not even met, so he cannot be too particular."

"Oh, I don't know about that. From what I know of
Wesleigh, I would say he is quite particular."

Emily looked up, startled. "You know Lord
Wesleigh?"

"Yes, we went to school together. And as I said, he is
quite particular in his tastes."

"Well, although I may not be as beautiful as Lydia, I
do not consider myself utterly repulsive."

"My dear, you cast your sister quite in the shade. I
think, from what I know of Wesleigh, you are much
more to his taste than she is."

"Am I?" Emily asked, although, at the present moment, her thoughts were not of Wesleigh's taste, but the man walking beside her. "You sound as if you know him quite well."

"I would say I know him rather well, yes."

"What is he like? What are his tastes, his interests?"

"Well, he is considered a likable gentleman, I suppose. Fairly popular."

"Yes, but what does he *do*? Does he travel, or is he political? Perhaps he's scholarly?"

"Well, no." Alexander was becoming a little uncomfortable. "He does what most gentlemen of his set do. You know, sporting pursuits, curricle races, that sort of thing."

"But those sound like the habits of a very young man. I thought he was close to thirty years of age."

"Yes, well, he has plans to lead a more purposeful sort of life. Become more involved in charitable works, institute improvements at his country estate, that kind of thing."

Under Emily's approving gaze Alexander wanted to rush right back to London and perform some worthwhile deed immediately, if only it meant she would continue to smile up at him in that manner.

"Do you know if he enjoys travel?"

Alexander thought for a moment. It was clear Emily desired to travel, and he wanted to answer her honestly. He had sincerely enjoyed his time on the Continent, but was inclined to stay in London, due to indolence more than anything else. Now he was struck by a burning desire to show Emily places like Italy and Greece, and see her big brown eyes light up with pleasure. That thought led to thoughts of other methods of making her eyes light up with pleasure, which he firmly suppressed since Emily was still awaiting his reply.

"I cannot say that Alexander and I have ever discussed whether or not he enjoys travel, but I am inclined to think he does. Particularly if he were to have with him a lovely traveling companion such as yourself."

Emily smiled. "Thank you, kind sir," she replied, with a mock curtsy, "but I wonder if you have been telling me the opinions of Lord Wesleigh or Mr. Williams."

Alexander "Williams" returned her curtsy with a bow, but did not reply. *They are one and the same, Emily,* he thought to himself. *They are one and the same.*

Five

೫೧൦ೕ

Emily returned home to be confronted by a furious Lydia. "Emily! Where were you? Mr. Sedgewick and I were forced to walk in circles in the hopes that you would catch up to us. When you did not come, Mr. Sedgewick was forced to escort me to the house, and Wiggins gave me *such* a look. I was quite ashamed, and poor Mr. Sedgewick did not know which way to look."

"Oh, pooh, Lydia. I do not know why you should concern yourself with what our butler thinks." Emily sounded confident, but she had turned a little red under Wiggins's disapproving gaze as well when she had shown up unchaperoned on Mr. Williams's arm. Thankfully he had been with the family long enough that they could trust him not to gossip.

"What took you so long, Emily? Mr. Sedgewick and I could not even see where you and Mr. Williams had gone."

"Oh, I twisted my ankle a little, and we were forced to walk slowly." Emily dismissed her sister's exclamations of concern with a wave of her hand. "Never mind me. Did you and Mr. Sedgewick have a nice time together?"

"Well, of course. I always enjoy Mr. Sedgewick's company. Although most of our conversation was taken up with where you had gone. I cannot imagine, Emily, that even with a twisted ankle, it took you so long to get home. Why, you are not even limping!"

"Never mind all that. I know, I know, it was wrong of me to leave you two alone together as I did. But did you talk of anything interesting? Did he pay you compliments, or attempt to court you at all?"

"Of course not! I hope you do not think, just because of my foolish infatuation, that Mr. Sedgewick returns my regard. He thinks of me only as another lamb in his flock."

"Only if he were a wolf. Do not talk such nonsense, Lydia. It is quite apparent that the gentleman is in love with you." Emily sincerely hoped she would be forgiven these little exaggerations in the interest of true love.

"What do you mean?" a pale Lydia asked. "Surely I have not betrayed my feelings in some manner. I would just die if he and I were the topic of local gossip."

"No, no, of course you are not. Perhaps I exaggerated a little." That, at least, was the truth. "I have been talking to Mr. Williams—"

"Emily! You have not betrayed my confidence to Mr. Williams! How could you?"

"Lydia, would you stop acting like the heroine of a bad tragedy! No, I did not betray your confidence. I did not have to. Mr. Williams noticed you and Mr. Sedgewick when you sang together the other evening, and mentioned that he thought Mr. Sedgewick had an interest in you but felt you were above his touch."

There was a pause, while Lydia assumed a tragic pose worthy of Sarah Siddons. "What nobility, what strength of character, to think that *I* am above *his* touch. It is *I* that am not worthy of *him.*"

Emily had never paid much attention to her sister's histrionic tendencies in the past. But today she was finding it quite wearing trying to anticipate what role Lydia would be playing next. Emily suppressed a sigh and tried to think which approach she should take. If she allowed Lydia to continue on in this vein, she would have Sedgewick and herself nobly sacrificing themselves for love, à la Romeo and Juliet. However, there would be no suicide; that would be far too vulgar. Lydia would probably just don wispy, fluttery clothing and mourn her lost love by heaving great sighs and peering out windows.

"Nonsense, Lydia." Emily decided to take the direct, sensible approach, although Lydia in love was the complete opposite. "You are perfect for each other. We just need to ensure that you are committed to each other prior to the marquess's arrival."

"Committed to each other? Whatever do you mean?"

Emily's patience was wearing thin. "You know, betrothed. Perhaps married. Some irrevocable commitment that would make it impossible for you to marry Lord Wesleigh."

"Married? Emily, he'll be here any day. How could we possibly be married prior to his arrival?"

"Oh, Lydia, I don't know. Hopefully you will not have to be. I just mentioned it as a last resort. But, if there is no other alternative, there's always Gretna Green."

As soon as the words were out of her mouth Emily knew she'd regret them. She had never before seen quite that expression of horror on her sister's face. Surprisingly, it did not detract from her beauty. Lydia's rosebud lips formed a perfect O, and her blue eyes widened attractively. Emily knew that if she tried to assume a similar expression, she would end up looking like a gargoyle. "Forget I even said anything about Gretna, Lydia. I am positive you will not need to elope. All we really need is to assure ourselves of Mr. Sedgewick's feelings toward you, and then we can explain the impossibility of your marriage to the marquess. Now, what will you wear to the assembly?"

ᔥᔦ

Alexander was having similar difficulties with Sedgewick. He, too, was furious about having been abandoned with Lydia.

"But I thought you enjoyed Miss Smithfield's company," Alexander exclaimed, the picture of innocence.

"Of course I do, she is a well-behaved young lady, but that does not answer the fact—"

"You do not have any interest in her beyond that?"

"I am not sure I understand. What do you mean by that question? My feelings toward the lady are entirely proper—"

"Yes, yes. I am sure they are," Alexander assured him, while racking his brain to think of a way to force a confession from someone so concerned with respectability. "However, Miss Emily Smithfield intimated to me that Miss Lydia Smithfield may have an interest in you beyond mere friendship."

"Miss Smithfield said that?" For a moment Jonathan Sedgewick allowed a look of amazed delight to cross his features, but it quickly turned into one of suspicion. "Why would she tell you that?"

"Apparently she thought that you may return her sister's feelings, and she was concerned that her sister might be forced into an arranged marriage with me."

"So she knows that you are actually Lord Wesleigh?"

"No, no, she doesn't know. I meant she is concerned that her sister might be forced into a marriage with Lord Wesleigh."

"Why would she confide in you her feelings if she did not know you were he?"

"Because she knew me to be your friend, and was hopeful that I could confirm that you returned her sister's regard." Alexander did not allow his exasperation to show on his face, but he wished his friend would just take him at his word and cease his interrogation.

His wish was granted. A look of bemusement crossed Sedgewick's face, and he grew so quiet Alexander thought he'd forgotten his presence. But, as Alexander watched him, he saw his friend's expression change from elation to despair. "It is useless even to hope," Sedgewick muttered.

"But, why? It's obvious you care for the lady, she returns your regard, the time-honored antidote for such a situation is marriage."

"But, her parent and your own wish for her to marry you. You have all the advantages, wealth, the title. What do I have to offer her? I cannot even compete."

"You do not have to," Alexander replied. "I withdraw from the competition. I have no desire to marry a lady who is in love with another. However, I find myself reluctant to try to explain to my father and Miss Smithfield's mother that as Lydia Smithfield is in love with another gentleman, I withdraw my suit. It would obviously be very embarrassing for the young lady with no proof that the gentleman in question returned her regard. Therefore, I need your assistance. You are going to have to put your luck to the touch at the local assembly."

৪০৫৪

Emily viewed her appearance in the mirror with approval. She knew that she was not up to London's fashion standards, and she wished she were able to wear more vibrant hues than an unmarried miss was allowed, but she was definitely in looks. She was wearing the palest of pinks, almost white, which suited her coloring better than darker pink or white. Her gown was cut simply, the neckline forming a deep V, almost meeting the riband of darker pink under her bust, and she had on the pearl necklace her father had given her shortly before his death. She was pleased to see that Lydia looked charming as well, and did not feel, as she sometimes did, that Lydia's appearance outshone her own. There was a happiness and excitement bubbling inside her that she felt nothing could dissipate.

Emily tried to convince herself that the excitement she felt was on Lydia's behalf, a sort of vicarious pleasure, but she knew it had much to do with the presence of a certain curate who behaved as if he were a lord.

She found him puzzling, a mystery that needed solving, and wanted desperately to believe that was her sole interest in the gentleman. She could not be falling in love with a penniless curate. What kind of life could they have together? He did not even have a living, no real means of supporting a wife. Her family was not rich, by any means, but they were not impoverished, either, which she would be were she to marry Mr. Williams. But what was intriguing about Mr. Williams was that he did not behave as if he were impoverished. There was no deference about him, no false humility. He did not kowtow to Lord or Lady Abernathy, but behaved as if he thought he was their equal. Although he and Sedgewick were friends, Sedgewick seemed almost to defer to Mr. Williams. It was very odd. Emily felt sure there was more to Mr. Williams than there appeared. And she was determined to find out what it was.

But that is my only interest in him, she assured herself. And found herself reassuring herself as soon as she saw him at the assembly that evening.

He was with Jonathan Sedgewick, who looked pale as a ghost. Emily was not sure if that was a good sign or a bad one. It probably meant that Mr. Williams had spoken with him about Lydia, as he'd promised, but Sedgewick looked more as a man does when presented with his worst nightmare, not his fondest dream. Did Sedgewick not return Lydia's regard?

Emily looked at her sister and was reassured when she saw that Lydia resembled a frightened rabbit. She knew Lydia was in love with Sedgewick. The two must both be suffering from nothing more than an attack of nerves. It was up to her and Williams to smooth the lovers' path. Her encouraging look in Williams's direction was enough to bring him promptly to her side, offering to lead her out in the first dance. When she accepted, leaving Sedgewick alone with Lydia, they had no choice but to join the set that was forming.

"They do not appear very eager, for two people in love," Alexander said in a low voice to Emily.

"I know. It is very odd. Perhaps they are both just shy. I am sure as the dance progresses they will warm up toward one another."

But as the dance progressed, Lydia and Sedgewick appeared to be going through the motions of the dance in utter silence. Sedgewick's face was rigid and taut; Lydia would barely raise her head. Emily, who was enjoying her dance with Williams immensely, was disturbed by her sister's odd behavior. Nonetheless, she whispered to Sedgewick as the motions of the dance brought them together: "Say something to her!"

Sedgewick looked affronted, turned red, and clamped his jaws together even tighter.

Emily sighed, and attempted to resume conversation with Mr. Williams, but noticed that he appeared distracted all of a sudden, and was barely managing intelligent replies to her attempts at conversation. She followed his gaze and was disappointed to see he was staring at Lady Abernathy's party, which had just arrived. His attention appeared to be riveted on a particular blond lady, who, even from this distance, looked to be outstandingly beautiful and fashionable. "Lady Cynthia, I presume."

"What?" Her partner replied, finally shaken out of his reverie.

"I presume that is Lady Cynthia you are craning your neck to get a glimpse of."

"I would not know, never having met the lady. However, I can assure you that I was not craning my neck to get a glimpse of her, as you so delicately termed my behavior. I have a far more stunning lady quite nearby, whose, ahem, charms are perfectly visible without requiring any neck-craning on my part."

Emily could tell from the direction of his gaze what particular charms he was referring to, and felt a blush forming in that general vicinity. However, she would not be taken in by his silver tongue. "What gammon. I bet you could tell me how many golden strands she had on her well-formed head."

"Ah, that is where you are wrong. Even if I was admiring the lady, I would not have been admiring her hair, as I have always preferred brunettes over blondes."

Before Emily could think of a response to that outrageous statement, the music ended, and she was being steered to the French doors that led to the terrace.

"Mr. Williams! Where are we going?"

"You look flushed. I thought you could use some fresh air."

Giving her no chance to respond, he propelled her outdoors. "Now, isn't this nice?" he asked Emily. Once again, though, he was not looking at her but was looking over her head into the assembly rooms. Emily tried to turn her head to see who or what had caught his attention and was pulled out of the light into the darker part of the gardens.

"Mr. Williams, what are you—" Before Emily could finish the sentence she had been pulled abruptly into Mr. Williams's arms, and he had covered her mouth with his own.

Emily's first thought was to struggle, which she did, putting her hands against his chest in an attempt to push him off. But his mouth on hers was gentle, unthreatening, and his hands on her waist were warm. She felt if she were being protected rather than assaulted, and she rather liked the feeling, so the hand she had raised to push him off curled around his neck and somehow ended up pulling him tighter.

Alexander had felt her first attempt at resistance and was wondering what he would have done if she had pulled away and slapped him across the face. There would have been no avoiding Lady Cynthia in that case, who had followed them to the French doors and had peered out into the gardens, looking for him. But Emily's initial resistance had turned into enthusiastic cooperation, and, after assuring himself that Lady Cynthia had returned to the assembly rooms without spotting them, he entered wholeheartedly into the embrace. Emily, who had just a moment earlier felt protected in his embrace, now felt that she was in the greatest danger of her life, as his lips, which had been gentle and tender, increased the pressure, and his hands, which had been resting casually at her waist, were somehow stroking her bare back and shoulders. Just as she was thinking she really needed to end the embrace, and yet how much she really did not want to, Alexander lifted his head.

"I really should apologize for my ungentlemanly behavior, but I cannot honestly say I am sorry." As Emily did not reply, but merely continued to stare at him, wide-eyed, Alexander laughed softly and kissed her on the tip of the nose. "I am afraid I must take my leave of you, Emily, but I am sure we will be meeting again shortly."

Emily gathered her scattered wits about her. "But where are you going? What about the rest of the assembly?"

"The rest of the evening would seem unbearably flat

in comparison with this experience, I assure you." So saying, he kissed the top of her head and disappeared into the gardens. Emily, after staring into the darkness a few minutes, slowly returned to the assembly rooms. All the excitement had faded from the evening. "He is right," she muttered to herself as she walked inside the doors and surveyed the scene before her. "The rest of the evening does seem unbearably flat."

She returned to her mother's side, to find her in conversation with Lady Abernathy. "I thought the poor dear would have wanted to rest after her experience, but she assured me she was fine, and did not want to cast a pall over the rest of the party," Lady Abernathy was telling her mother. "She even condescended to come to this assembly, although I'm sure after the fetes and balls of London this seems a sad comedown."

"Emily," Lady Smithfield addressed her daughter, "poor Lady Cynthia Sommers, Lady Abernathy's niece, was attacked by a highwayman en route from London this morning."

"How awful," Emily replied. "She was not hurt, I trust."

"No, no, although I fear the dreadful man may have tried to take liberties with her." Lady Abernathy lowered her voice. "I believe he attempted to embrace her."

"No!" Lady Smithfield said, in shocked accents. "How disgusting. Why, I do not know how I would react if a brigand treated one of my girls in such a shocking manner."

Emily wondered what her reaction would be if she knew that Emily had just been in a similar situation with a curate. Probably the same as if she had been embraced by a highwayman. Lady Smithfield viewed highwaymen and impoverished curates as being on about the same rung of the social ladder.

"Yes, poor Cynthia. Thankfully she has a great deal of fortitude. Ah, it appears she is coming this way now. Let me introduce you both to my niece, Lady Cynthia Sommers."

The introductions were duly made, and Lady Abernathy and Lady Smithfield continued in conversation, leaving Emily and Lady Cynthia to converse. Emily did not have much of a desire to converse with Lady Cynthia, as she appeared even more haughty and disdainful up close than she did from afar. However, it appeared that Lady Cynthia did wish to talk with Emily.

"Miss Smithfield, I happened to notice the gentleman you were dancing the last set with, and he reminded me quite forcibly of an acquaintance of mine, but he seems to have disappeared. The last I saw of him he appeared to have entered the gardens."

Emily tried with all her might not to do anything or say anything that might appear guilty or suspicious, because from the accusatory look Lady Cynthia was giving her, even if she did not observe Emily's behavior on the terrace, she appeared to suspect her of misbehavior all the same.

"Oh, do you know Mr. Williams? He specifically mentioned that he had not made your acquaintance. I am surprised you would number a country curate among your acquaintances, Lady Cynthia. But then again, he is rather distinguished-looking, even for a curate, is he not?"

"A curate, you say? No, I suppose I have not made

his acquaintance after all. Although he did look suspiciously like . . . Oh, well. I guess it's as you mentioned. He does present a distinguished appearance, even for a curate."

One of Lady Abernathy's party came to request Lady Cynthia's hand for a dance shortly after this exchange, and Emily danced most of the evening as well. However, the conversation she'd had with Lady Cynthia continued to haunt her for a long time afterward. Mr. Williams had been paying close attention to Lady Cynthia, even though he claimed not to know her, and he had been observing someone even after he and Emily had left the assembly rooms. Lady Cynthia, by her own admission, had seen them go out onto the terrace. Had Williams been attempting to avoid Lady Cynthia? Is that why he pulled her into the shadows and embraced her? Was it just a ploy, to avoid discovery by Lady Cynthia?

The more Emily thought about it, the more she was sure that Williams had been avoiding Lady Cynthia. He had become distracted the minute her party arrived, and he had ushered Emily out onto the terrace without a word of explanation, yanked her into the shadows, and kissed her, and then disappeared into the gardens without even a good-bye to his friend Sedgewick. She found herself growing more and more infuriated by the minute. Her first kiss, which had seemed so sweet and passionate, was nothing more than a prop in his scene with Lady Cynthia. She had meant nothing more to him than a hedge that he could hide behind.

"That cad! That disgusting libertine!" Emily said under her breath, startling a gentleman who had approached her to ask her for the next dance. He looked bewildered and turned to Lydia instead, so Emily was free to pursue her own thoughts. She would never speak to Williams again. If he tried to approach her, she would give him the cut direct. She amused herself for a few minutes picturing the bewildered, hurt expression on his face as she proudly refused to recognize him, before realizing that that was a sorry revenge indeed. If she cut him, and never spoke to him again, how would she ever find out what secret he was hiding? Her best revenge would be to reveal his masquerade to the world and watch him reap his just deserts. Yes, that was it. She would solve the mystery of Alexander Williams, for she was sure that whatever it was he was playing at, he was up to no good.

Six

⧬)(⧬

Jonathan Sedgewick, who was already wishing his first guest anywhere but his own previously peaceful abode, was amazed to receive yet another unexpected visitor. This one, however, did not arrive by public coach. He arrived in a luxurious traveling carriage, with another carriage following behind him with servants and baggage. Jonathan and Alexander, who were taking their ease in the library, heard the commotion and looked at each other in confusion. Before Jonathan could rise from his chair, an apparition appeared in the doorway.

The gentleman was blinding. From his flaxen hair to his shiny Hessians, everything about him was beaming. He was wearing a turquoise jacket of exquisite cut, with a canary yellow waistcoat covered in rosebuds. The huge diamond in his cravat reflected the many colors of his ensemble. "Don't bother to get up, Sedgewick," the apparition said, "it is Wesleigh I am here to see."

"Hullo, Marcus. How did you find me?" Alexander asked, unperturbed.

"The estimable Jenkins. He was quite upset, old man, that you would leave him in London and descend upon the wilds of Stonehurst with no one to see to your sartorial well-being." Marcus examined Alexander through his quizzing glass. "I see his fears were well-founded."

"Cut line, Marcus. What are you doing here?"

"I am pretending to be you."

"What?" Alexander bellowed, jumping up from his seat.

"Your pater told me you had gone to Stonehurst to court a young lady, but then Jenkins told me you went on the public stage, leaving him and the best portion of your wardrobe behind. Simmons mentioned Sedgewick, I put two and two together, and *voilà*! I came out with four."

"Is that an explanation? It sounds as though you put two and two together and came out with forty-six. What led you to think you should come masquerade as me?"

"I am *persona non grata* right now in London. I need to make myself scarce for a few days, perhaps a sennight. I figured you were pretending to be someone else, why shouldn't I pretend to be you? By the way, just exactly who, or what, are you supposed to be?" The quizzing glass reappeared, as if it could help Marcus decipher Alexander's identity.

"I am a curate."

"Hmmm. Well, if you would prefer, you could go back to being Lord Wesleigh, and I could be the curate."

Sedgewick looked quite alarmed at this notion; if Alexander had been irritating as a guest, what was he in for with Sir Marcus Reddings, dandy *extraordinaire*? However, Alexander just laughed. "You, a curate?"

Marcus appeared affronted. "I will have you know, Alexander, that my grandmother was a fine actress in her day. Of course, that is all very hush-hush. Mater wouldn't like that old business hashed up again, but it's in the blood, nonetheless, it's in the blood. I could probably give a more than creditable sermon this Sunday, if Sedgewick wanted the morning off."

"I am sure Sedgewick appreciates the offer, but I think not," Alexander replied. "I prefer to remain incognito for a little longer, myself."

"Petticoat trouble, *n'est-çe pas?* Well, that leads me back to my original offer. I will be you."

"But you cannot be me. I am supposed to be staying with Lady Smithfield and offering for her daughter. I do not believe that your need for privacy is so great that you are willing to sacrifice yourself on the marriage altar."

"That would depend," Sir Marcus responded, casually observing his fingernails. "Just what does Miss Smithfield look like?"

Sedgewick bristled, but Alexander just laughed. He had learned not to take Marcus Reddings seriously. He understood his need for privacy, as well. Marcus acted like a brainless fop, but it was just that, an act. He occasionally did some governmental work that included spying. He was well connected, and no one took him seriously, so he was able to ferret out quite a few secrets.

"Sorry, old friend, I would like to help, but Stonehurst has become a veritable beehive of activity these past few days. Lady Cynthia Sommers is here, as well as Farnwright, and I do not know how many others. It would never work. They all know me and you."

"But I do not plan on socializing. Can't you tell I have a horrible case of the grippe?"

Marcus looked healthy as a horse. "Even if you tell them you have the grippe, how do I explain to them when the jig is over that I allowed you to pose as me?"

Alexander asked.

"You were testing your young lady's love for you. If she could fall in love with you as a lowly curate, she passes the test. Otherwise, she's failed. Any woman with blood in her veins will fall for that one. It's the kind of claptrap they fill their heads with in those silly Gothic romances they all read."

Since that was precisely how he was going to explain his deception, and the reason he was going through all of this in the first place, he could not argue that point. He also wondered what Emily would do if faced with Marcus as a potential husband. Would she go through with her plans to marry the heir of a duke?

He realized that at some point in the midst of the game he was playing the rules had changed. He no longer cared to discover Lydia Smithfield's true character. He was relieved she was as unwilling to marry him as he was to marry her. But, somehow, in the course of this charade he had begun to care about Emily Smithfield's true character. He found himself entranced by her big brown eyes and vivacious manner. And, if the truth were told, that kiss was quite beguiling as well, to say the very least. But he was stymied by her announcement that she planned to marry Lord Wesleigh. He was beginning to think all he wanted was to marry Emily Smithfield, sweep her away to Venice or Rome, show her London and show London to her. But some romantic part of his soul that he did not know even existed wanted her to fall in love with himregardless of his position or rank. So he had persisted in the charade, even though he knew it was no longer necessary. He had no doubt that his father would not force him into marriage with a lady who was in love with another gentleman. He could return to London to-day and explain the situation to his father and be free. It was as simple as that. But he was no longer free. He would leave a portion of himself there in Stonehurst, with her. Really, Marcus would be doing him a favor by pretending to be Lord Wesleigh. If Emily still persisted in wanting to wed the heir of a duke, no matter who he was, then, as hard a fact as that was to swallow, she would have made her choice.

He looked up from his deliberation to find Marcus looking at him expectantly, almost sympathetically. "That bad, is it?" Marcus asked, his voice pitched low so Jonathan could not overhear. "I must say I am glad Cupid hasn't yet struck me with any of his little pointy arrows. It appears they sting quite a bit." Raising his voice, he asked: "So after all that cogitation, what decision have you reached? Am I to assist our noble vicar in his duties? Or warm a bed at Lady Smithfield's house, my frail body wracked by shuddering coughs?"

Before Sedgewick could start sputtering again, Alexander replied, "It looks to me like you should take to your bed immediately. You appear to have contracted a serious case of the grippe."

§Ọ꒰

The gentlemen settled down to make plans. It appeared Marcus had apprehended Alexander's traveling carriage while in London. It was a simple matter of having his servants address Sir Marcus as Lord Wesleigh, and that should be all that was necessary, as long as Marcus did not leave the house and did not accept visitors. The only visitor he would accept would be Alexander, who had already told Emily he was acquainted with Lord Wesleigh. When Sedgewick left the room, Alexander clued Marcus in on the true state of affairs, explaining which of the Smithfield daughters he was interested in.

"I love it," Marcus said, after having heard the whole story. "It has all the elements of a French farce. All we need is a jealous husband."

"I could do without that complication," Alexander replied. "So, how long should your business take?"

"Hopefully no more than a few days. There has been a highwayman causing a great deal of commotion in the area. I am here to apprehend him."

"Yes, I have heard talk of him. He has the local ladies all aflutter. They are going to start lining up to be robbed by him if there is any more gossip about his lovemaking. He even managed to get a kiss from that iceberg Lady Cynthia."

"That is an accomplishment," Marcus said. "Do I detect a note of jealousy in your voice?"

"Well, you know I do not take defeat very well. Little did I know that all I had to do to steal a kiss from her was put on a mask and say 'Stand and deliver.'" Both men laughed, before growing serious once more.

"I do not understand your involvement in this affair. Is not this a job for the local constable?" Alexander asked.

"It seems our highwayman is interested in more than jewelry. It appears he has somehow discovered the route our messenger takes when delivering assignments to the troops on the coast. He has been intercepting them and selling the information to the French. We want to discover who else is working with him."

Alexander nodded. "I would be happy to assist you in whatever way I can." Marcus thanked him for the offer, but reiterated that what he needed most was a place to stay. "Well, I guess Smithfield House is as good a place as any to hide out in for a few days. No one in that household should recognize you."

Except, of course, the duke of Alford, who was en route to Stonehurst as they spoke.

ഇൻരു

The ladies of Smithfield House had heard the carriages arrive, and were sitting in the drawing room, awaiting the announcement of their distinguished guest. They assumed, it being Tuesday, the day he had written he would be coming, that the duke of Alford would be announced. There was a moment of stunned silence when Wiggins stated in a triumphant tone of voice, "Lord Wesleigh." Wiggins knew his mistresses were expecting someone else, and it pleased him to surprise them. He always prided himself on knowing more about what was going on in the household than anyone else, even the mistress.

The ladies may have been able to recover themselves sooner if it were not for the strange sight that greeted them when "Lord Wesleigh" walked in the room. Marcus had changed his outfit to one he thought would better suit his new role. He felt a person in the full throes of the grippe should dress in a more subdued manner. To that end, he had discarded his turquoise and yellow, deciding in favor of puce and gray, with a paisley waistcoat. In order to give the impression that the sunlight was too harsh for his weakened eyesight, he was wearing a pair of green glasses. He held a handkerchief over his mouth and was feebly coughing into it as he walked into the room.

Lady Smithfield was the first to recover. "Lord Wesleigh, what a pleasant surprise, please sit down." She tried to approach him to lead him over to a chair, but when she got closer he backed up, waving her away.

"Lady Smithfield, I beg your pardon"—cough, cough—"but I am quite ill. Please do not come any closer, we do not want to risk contagion."

"Oh, yes, of course." Lady Smithfield retreated to her seat, racking her brain to try and remember the proper etiquette to follow when one had a guest who had a mysterious illness and would not allow one to approach him.

"I think that I shall be forced to spend the next few days in my room, until I recover from this humiliating illness. Perhaps, once I have been introduced to your charming daughters, you could conduct me to my room?"

"Of course, of course. Girls, come make your curtsy to Lord Wesleigh." As Lord Wesleigh almost backed into one of the tables as the girls approached, Lady Smithfield hurriedly reminded them, "Not too close, mind."

Lord Wesleigh pronounced himself charmed to meet first Lydia and then Emily. He started to lift his quizzing glass to peruse the girls more closely, when he saw Emily struggling to keep from giggling. Then he remembered the green glasses he was wearing. Never one to fear ridicule, he raised his quizzing glass anyway, and received a magnified view of Emily's sparkling brown eyes, through a green haze.

The sight appeared to be too much for Lord Wesleigh. He dropped his quizzing glass, shuddered, and in a weak voice, asked, "My chamber?"

"Of course, my lord, Lydia will direct you to your chamber. Lydia, show Lord Wesleigh to the Green Suite, please."

Lydia, who appeared just as pale as Lord Wesleigh, nonetheless followed her mother's dictum. She left the room, Lord Wesleigh following. At the doorway of his chamber, feeling compelled to say something, she mentioned that he must be pleased his father would be arriving soon.

"What's that? My father?" Marcus asked in stronger tones then he had employed thus far.

"Why, yes, he is to arrive today, is he not?" Lydia asked.

"Of course, of course. Just so." Lydia left him, and Marcus took off his glasses and began a hurried note to Alexander "Williams," which he dispatched with one of the servants to be delivered to the vicarage.

めCみ

Soon after Lord Wesleigh's arrival, Emily took a maid and went for a walk in the village. She had no real errands, but wanted an excuse to get out of the house. She felt after meeting the marquess that she had some thinking to do.

She did not want to admit to herself how disappointed she was with the marquess. She realized now that she had been deceiving herself all along. She had thought, when she offered to marry the marquess in her sister's stead, that she was being practical and reasonable.

Now she realized that she had been hoping the whole time that the marquess would turn out to be someone she could love and respect. "A knight in shining armor," she muttered disgustedly to herself. She had been as impractical and unreasonable as it is possible for a silly, romantical nineteen-year-old girl to be.

She knew as soon as she saw the marquess that she would not marry him. And she knew Lydia should not be forced to do so, either. So they were in a proper fix. Lydia, if she were allowed, would marry a vicar, and Emily would be maiden aunt to all their little blue-eyed babies. That was a far cry from the life of travel and excitement she'd dreamed of for herself. Unless, of course, she were to marry a certain curate . . .

Emily shook her head. He was a dastardly knave, toying with her affections and who knew what else. She was convinced he was not a curate at all. He wore a ring on his fifth finger that was probably worth a curate's salary for the entire year. She didn't know what he was up to, but the more she thought on the matter, the more she was convinced there was something not quite right about Mr. Williams. Unfortunately, there were times when she felt that there was everything right about Mr. Williams.

She sighed and,, looking up, saw the man she had just been daydreaming about walking toward her. It was the first time she'd encountered him since their kiss, and she felt her cheeks coloring in memory. He smiled at her; really, it was almost a smirk, as if he knew what she was thinking.

"May I walk with you, Emily?"

Emily nodded, although all her instincts were telling her to flee, to run away as fast as she could from this man, with his twinkling brown eyes and mysterious behavior. She noticed he had called her Emily more than once now, and although she had not given him leave to call her by her first name, she had to admit she enjoyed hearing it on his lips. She would have also felt quite ridiculous making an issue of it, when she had allowed him the greater familiarity of embracing her.

"I wanted to apologize for my abrupt departure the other evening."

Although Emily's cheeks now felt as if they were on fire, since his words could not help but recall their actions directly prior to his departure, she felt this would be the perfect opportunity to get some answers to the questions that were plaguing her. "It did seem rather sudden. I could not help but think you were avoiding Lady Cynthia for some reason."

"Now what reason would I have for avoiding such a beautiful young lady?"

"That is exactly my question, sir. She said afterward that she thought she recognized you." Emily looked up at Alexander, fixing him with an accusatory glance she felt sure would signify to him that she knew he was up to something. To her dismay, he just laughed, and said, "My nanny always told me that everybody has a double somewhere. It appears Lady Cynthia has encountered mine. Now let us quit this subject. I find that when I am with you, I have no desire to discuss other young ladies. Do you not have any shopping to do, so that I will be forced to carry your parcels for you?"

"No, I should really be returning home."

"Yes," Alexander replied, removing a speck of lint from his sleeve, "I hear you have a guest in residence."

"How did you—"

"News spreads quickly in a small village such as this. So what did you think of the marquess?"

Emily found herself reluctant to discuss the subject with Mr. Williams. "He seemed polite enough, I suppose. He certainly did not fit your description of him."

"I was not aware that I gave a description of him."

"Well, perhaps not, but you could have at least mentioned his tendency toward—" Emily paused, seeking the most politic word.

"Yes?" Alexander prompted.

"Well, he seems to be rather given to dramatic effect."

"Perhaps you are right. I thought you were more interested in his pocketbook than his character."

Emily looked reproachfully at Alexander, the hurt evident in her expression. "I think I would prefer to walk alone."

"Emily, I am sorry. I did not mean that. I was just jealous. It was a rotten thing to say, and I apologize. Can you forgive me?"

The word "jealous" had the amazing effect of making her forget that he was hiding some dreadful secret and was a dangerous man. She just knew that she, Emily Smithfield, was capable of making this gorgeous creature jealous. It was a delightful sensation, and in the afterglow of that remark she would forgive him practically anything. However, in the next moment he did something that brought all the doubts and anxiety rushing back.

They had neared the end of the High Street, when they heard the sound of a carriage approaching. Emily, looking over her shoulder, noticed the coat of arms was the same as that on Lord Wesleigh's carriage. However, before she had an opportunity to say so to the gentleman walking beside her he had disappeared. She looked all around, but she did not see him anywhere. In desperation, she called to her maid: "Bess, did you see where the gentleman I was walking with went?"

"No, miss, I was watching the carriage. Did he go off and leave you?"

"It appears so. Never mind, let's go home."

୫୦୪

Alexander did not know what course to take. His initial reaction was to hide, lest his father recognize him, but as he recovered from his surprise, he wondered if he should just confess all and call it quits. Then again, he was no longer the only one involved in this masquerade—there was Reddings to consider as well. Alexander walked back to the vicarage slowly, weighing his options. When he arrived, he was handed the message from Reddings informing him that his father was on his way to Stonehurst.

"Thanks for the warning, old chap, but you are a little late," Alexander mumbled to himself. He crumpled the note in his hand, standing and thinking for a moment. He finally shrugged and went to the library to read. There was little he could do but wait. It was up to Reddings to carry the day. Alexander would find out soon enough if the masquerade was at an end, and if he went bumbling into the Smithfield's house with his father sitting in the drawing room, he was liable to do more harm than good. No, he would wait. And if he did not hear anything by nightfall, he would contact Reddings surreptitiously under cover of darkness.

கை

Emily returned to the house, irritated once more by Williams's cryptic behavior. This was the second time he had disappeared in the middle of a conversation, and she was more determined than ever to find out what reason there was for his bizarre actions. She wanted nothing more than to go to her bedchamber to think, but her mother called out to her from the drawing room as she walked by.

"Emily, come make your curtsy to His Grace, the duke of Alford."

Emily did not even have time to check a mirror, and hoped the walk had not left her hair in disarray. She patted it nervously, walking into the drawing room. She saw a distinguished-looking man of middle age, above average in height. He was a little thick around the waist, but other than that and the gray mixed in with his dark hair, he looked remarkably well for a man with a thirty-year-old son. He had arisen upon Emily's entrance, and she sank into a curtsy before him.

"Well, well, Lady Smithfield. You are blessed indeed. Two beautiful daughters. I see now why you choose to rusticate in the country rather than bring them to London. You would be the envy of every mother with a marriageable daughter." The duke smiled kindly at Emily, and she smiled back. She had expected a male version of Lady Abernathy and was pleased to find that he was not arrogant at all.

Lady Smithfield giggled in response to the duke's little sally, thanking him for the kind compliment, before turning to Emily and telling her that His Grace would be retiring to his room shortly, as he had been attacked by a highwayman on the journey down from London and wanted to rest a bit before dinner.

Before Emily had a chance to respond, Lady Smithfield continued, "Really, I cannot think what the world is coming to these days. You are the second person I know who has been the victim of that highwayman in the past week. Perhaps you know Lady Cynthia Sommers? Her carriage was attacked as well. It really is a shame. But I won't keep you from your bed. Bess will show you to your room. As I mentioned earlier, Lord Wesleigh is staying in the suite right next door. Such a shame he won't be joining us for dinner, but he said he would not be feeling well enough and requested a tray in his room."

Lydia had been sitting quietly through the whole exchange, but roused herself to smile at the duke as he left, although the smile trembled at the edges.

The duke decided to check on his son after being shown to his room. He had been surprised to hear Alexander was ill. Even when Alexander was sick, he never played the invalid, as he hated for a fuss to be made over him. The duke hoped Alexander was not up to some lark at his hostess's expense, but really could not think what could be gained by pretending to be sick. He went to the chamber next to his that had been pointed out to him by the maid and knocked quietly at the door. After hearing a feeble, "Come in," the duke entered his son's chamber.

"Alexander, it's your father," the duke said, approaching the figure on the bed huddled under a mass of blankets. "I was sorry to hear that you are ill. Should a doctor be sent for?"

Marcus realized he could not hide under a pile of blankets forever. Besides, it was hot as Hades under there. "Good afternoon, Your Grace. Sorry to surprise you like this, but I can explain everything."

The duke appeared more resigned than surprised to see Sir Marcus Reddings's head pop out of the bed-clothes, not a flaxen hair out of place.

"I am sure you can, Sir Marcus. And, I must admit, I am somewhat interested in hearing your explanation. I will just take a seat, shall I, while you prepare your, no doubt fascinating, account." As the duke's tone was laden with sarcasm and his gaze somewhat fierce, it is not surprising that Sir Marcus felt a hint of trepidation and a loss of some of his usual savoir-faire. "*I should have been the curate*," he said under his breath, but launched into his explanation before the duke forced him to explain that cryptic utterance.

"I am sure Alexander would do a better job of explaining to you his motives, but I will do my poor best to explain them in his absence." Marcus paused, but as the duke's only response was a glare, he hurried to continue. "Yes, well, Alexander felt that if he came to Stonehurst as the heir to a duke known to be promised in marriage to Miss Smithfield, there would be no opportunity for him and Miss Smithfield to come to know each other's real characters. So he decided to come to Stonehurst incognito, so to speak, and get to know Miss Smithfield in a less formal atmosphere. So he is presently residing with the vicar of Stonehurst, posing as a curate."

"My son is posing as a curate."

"That is right, Your Grace, but with the purest of

motives, I assure you."

"So you have said. I hope the Church of England appreciates the nobility of his actions as much as you do. But while I can comprehend my son's behavior, as much as I abhor the deceit, it still does not explain why you are posing as him."

"That is true. Really, it is because of your son's generosity that I am here."

"No sophistry, I beg you. Just cut to the chase."

"I needed to leave London and did not really have anywhere to go. I discovered that Alexander had come here posing as a curate. That left his identity free, so I assumed it. I cannot go into detail about my reasons, but they are good ones, Your Grace." There was more sincerity in Marcus's tone than usual, and he had dropped his foppish façade. The duke observed him in silence for a long moment, then nodded.

"I am not saying I condone your actions; I detest falsehood. However, I accept your explanation."

"Does that mean that you will go along with the charade?"

"I shan't be a party to it, but I shall not expose you, either. As long as you stay in your chamber, and I do not have to address you in public, and Alexander stays out of my sight, you both can continue your game. But I give you one week only. I will not deceive my hostess and her family any longer than that."

Sir Marcus nodded acceptance of the duke's terms. "You know, Your Grace, Alexander and I had no idea you were coming. When Miss Smithfield told me today you were expected, you could have knocked me over with a feather. I am sure Alexander was equally surprised when he got my note."

"I think he was surprised even before he got your note, young man. I saw him walking on the High Street with Miss Emily Smithfield, and he ran into the butcher's when he saw my carriage." The duke started to laugh. "I should have stopped my carriage and ordered some mutton. I wonder what he would have done then."

Seven

ഇറെ

The duke had just dismissed his man and retired for the night when he heard the door to his chamber open and close. Before he could react, someone had placed a hand over his mouth and whispered to him to be still. The hand was removed, and the duke was considering crying for help despite the warning, when the candle at his bedside was lit and he saw his son standing above him.

"Alexander! Are you trying to give me an apoplexy?"

"No, sir, I apologize, but I did not want you waking the whole house."

"I swear, your shenanigans are going to send me to an early grave."

"I know, I know, I am a sad excuse for a son. You deserve a son more like . . . Sir Marcus Reddings, perhaps?"

"That is very amusing, Alexander. Very amusing."

"I am sorry, sir. I know it is not a matter to joke about, and I apologize for involving you in this. However, I have a very good explanation for it all."

"I know, I know. Sir Marcus explained the whole thing. It is all very romantic. I only hope the Smithfields are still speaking to us when the whole thing is over."

"So do I." Alexander's tone was so serious that his

father looked at him more closely.

"Why do you care so much for the Smithfields' good opinion all of a sudden? Could it be you have come to appreciate Miss Smithfield's sterling qualities?"

"I do admire Miss Smithfield's sterling qualities. However, I find Miss Emily Smithfield's more, ahem, corporal qualities practically irresistible."

The duke smiled at his son's admission. "I must admit, I spent the entire evening at dinner wondering if I had engaged you to the right girl."

"So you approve my choice?"

"I am delighted. However, I cannot understand why you're resorting to these underhanded tactics. It all seems like a lot of unnecessary tomfoolery. Why can't things be like they were in my day? You saw a pretty girl you liked, good family, asked permission to court her, that's that. I feel like a dashed idiot, accepting hospitality from a woman I am playing for a fool."

"I know, Father, and I apologize again for putting you in this position. But, whatever the reason I started this charade, I want to finish it for a different reason. I know Emily Smithfield is the right girl for me. But she is very young, and I do not want her head turned by the attentions of the heir to a dukedom. I want to know that she chooses to spend the rest of her life with me for the same reason I choose to spend it with her: because she could not bear not to."

"Well, I do not pretend to understand young people today, it seems to me you waste a lot of time and energy playing games when all you have to do is talk to each other. But I shan't stand in your way. If you want to go round in circles, that is your prerogative."

"Thank you, sir. Now you shall have a far more entertaining story to tell your grandchildren."

"The way you are going about things, I am unlikely to see any grandchildren. Now go away, I have had a long day and need my sleep."

"Yes, I heard you had an encounter with a highwayman this afternoon. Are you all right?"

"I am fine, he only hurt my dignity. It pained me to give the young whippersnapper my money. However, I always travel with a little extra in my boot, so I will survive. And if I need any more, I can always ask one of my sons for a loan."

"Good night, Father. I can see you're perfectly fine." Alexander turned to go.

"Alexander, one more thing. I gave your friend Marcus one week only. I do not want to have to claim that dandy as my son for the rest of my life. I hate to give advice to a young Lothario like you, but you may want to speed things up a bit. Meet her in dark corners, bribe the maid to disappear . . ."

"Steal a kiss on a dark terrace, I understand. Despite your lack of confidence in my abilities, I am not a complete novice, you know."

"Well, I had heard otherwise, but I am beginning to think the reports were highly exaggerated."

"Thank you, Father. Good night."

Alexander peeked out from behind the door to ensure no one was in the hallway and slipped out of the room. His father chuckled softly to himself before extinguishing the light.

Emily had been reading a Gothic before bed and

could not sleep. Every time she started to doze off, she would hear some suspicious sound that caused her to bolt upright. She tried to convince herself it was only in her head, but that last noise had sounded remarkably like a creaking door. *Fine. I'll prove it to you,* she told herself, lighting a candle and getting out of bed. *It is all in your head.* She opened her door and looked into the hall, just in time to see Alexander turn the corner.

She almost gasped at the sight of a strange man in her house, but the glimpse she had of him looked like Mr. Williams, so out of curiosity she decided to follow. He was moving very quickly, and ran down the stairs and out the back door before she could catch up with him, but as he ran out of the house the moon shone brightly on his face and she was sure it was he.

As she walked back up the stairs she wondered why Alexander Williams would be sneaking around her house. Really, none of his behavior made any sense whatsoever. First, he avoided Lady Cynthia, then, apparently, the duke of Alford, as she had come to the conclusion that was what had caused Alexander's strange disappearance on High Street earlier that afternoon. Yet he did not avoid Lord and Lady Abernathy or Jonathan Sedgewick. What did Lady Cynthia and the duke of Alford have in common that made him run at the sight of them?

Except, of course, that they had both been victims of a highwayman. It hit Emily with all the force of a blow to the stomach. Alexander's strange behavior, his expensive ring, and the fact that he acted nothing like a curate. His avoidance of Lady Cynthia and the duke of Alford, who could quite possibly recognize him and identify him. Alexander was the highwayman.

"No, it cannot be true," Emily told herself, sitting down on the edge of her bed. "I will not believe it."

But what other explanation was there? He was probably at their house tonight in an attempt to steal from them as well. They were not rich, but there were a few expensive paintings that had not been part of the entail, and her mother had some nice pieces of jewelry that had been gifts from Emily's father. That would explain Williams's surreptitious behavior, sneaking out of the house. He was nothing more than a common criminal.

"No, there must be some other explanation." Emily tried dearly to think of one. But it all fit; the highwayman's attacks had started about the same time as Alexander's appearance in the neighborhood, his manner was not at all that of a curate's, and he had made no attempt since coming to Stonehurst to seek out a permanent living. Added to that was his avoidance of his victims and his strange behavior tonight. What other conclusion could she reach?

Also, there were the descriptions given of the highwayman: "A gentleman fallen on hard times," "very gallant," "he attempted to embrace Lady Cynthia." That sounded just like Alexander. Stealing a kiss as he performed his "very gallant" thievery. "How could this be? How could I have fallen in love with a common thief?" Emily whispered to herself.

No—she shook her head—*I am not in love with him. I refuse to love him, I am infatuated, that is all.* She had known him less than a fortnight, and knew hardly more than his name. She had never been in love, but was sure love was born out of common experiences and interests, not physical attraction or because a pair of dark brown eyes looked at you as if you were the only person in the universe.

She was surprised to find, however, that infatuation hurt so very much. Almost as if her heart were breaking.

ഇന്ദ

In the cold light of day, Emily's suspicions of the previous night did not seem quite as credible, and she was not as convinced as she had been when she went to sleep that Alexander was the highwayman. But she still felt it probable, and determined to investigate the matter further. So she was pleased when the duke joined her at the breakfast table. Here was an excellent opportunity to quiz him about his meeting with the highwayman.

Unfortunately, the duke appeared to be one of those gentlemen who did not appreciate conversation at the breakfast table. After smiling at Emily and wishing her a good morning he seemed more than content to bury himself in the newspaper that he'd brought with him into the room. Emily was used to such behavior, as her late father had behaved in a similar manner. And she herself was not at her best in the morning, either. However, she felt a sense of urgency to discover the truth about Alexander Williams, and she might not have many other opportunities to question the duke.

"Excuse me, Your Grace?" It was tentatively said, and the duke did not appear annoyed by the interruption, as he just set aside the paper with a smile.

"I apologize, Miss Smithfield, I suppose I have grown accustomed to eating alone in the morning. A man can develop very bad habits when left to his own devices."

"Oh, no, Your Grace, I understand perfectly, my father always enjoyed reading the paper with his coffee. I will not interrupt you for very long. I just wanted to ask you if you felt you would recognize the highwayman if you were to see him again."

"What an odd question. What makes you ask such a thing?"

"Oh, just idle curiosity."

"Well, to answer your question, he was wearing a mask, of course, so his features were hidden, but if I were to hear him speak, I might recognize him. He was a cocky fellow, and spoke almost with the accent of a gentleman. Seemed above average in height and appeared to have dark hair. I have given all these details to the magistrate, of course, but it sounds as if you have decided to do a little investigating on your own. Please be very careful, Miss Smithfield. This is a serious business."

"Oh, no, as I said, it is only idle curiosity. I only wanted to know so that if I saw someone who fit the description, I could alert the authorities."

"There is no harm in that, I suppose. However, I doubt you will recognize someone merely by my description of him. He did not have any outstanding characteristics, unfortunately. Now, if he was a hunchback with a peg leg, or red hair, then he would stand out in a crowd."

"Yes, indeed," Emily responded, smiling. "Although I doubt such a man would have a successful career as a highwayman."

The duke laughed, and the subject was closed. Emily was greatly relieved, as she did not want to explain her interest in the highwayman to the duke. She should have known better to approach the subject as she did. It would have been less obvious had she brought the conversation round to the topic.

Lady Smithfield and Lydia came into the room together, Lydia still appearing greatly subdued and Lady Smithfield more than compensating for her daughter's lack of animation. She could barely keep from shouting in triumph, "A duke at my breakfast table!" She managed to contain herself, however, and instead asked the duke if he had enjoyed a good night's rest.

"Yes, thank you. I was exceedingly comfortable."

"Good, good. Have you and your son any plans for the day?" Lady Smithfield asked.

"What's that? Alexander? No, we have no plans to do anything together. I believe he plans to keep to his room. He is still suffering from his illness."

"Such a shame. I understand just how he feels. My constitution is rather delicate as well. I do hope, however, that he will permit us to entertain him. Lydia has a very soothing voice in a sickroom, and she would be more than willing to read to him."

Lydia looked less than willing, but did not object, and the duke hurried to assure Lady Smithfield that would be the very thing. "For Alexander is bound to get restless, staring at the walls all day, and if I had to hazard a guess, I would say he's going to be laid up with his malady for at least a week."

"Really? Does he usually contract the grippe for a week at a time?"

"Practically to the minute. And at the end of the week, he is so improved you would not even recognize him. He is a different person altogether," the duke stated in such an odd tone that Emily looked suspiciously at him. He noticed her observing him, and she could have sworn he winked.

"Well, then, Lydia will entertain Lord Wesleigh, but that leaves you at loose ends, Your Grace. 'Tis a pity Sir John is no longer with us. However, if you would like, Emily and I would be more than happy to show you the local sights."

"My dear lady, do not trouble yourself. I believe Lord Abernathy lives in the vicinity, does he not?" At Lady Smithfield's assurance that he did, he continued, "There is a bill up for debate in the House that I'd like to discuss with him, so I arranged to call on him today. I will have plenty to keep me occupied the next week, I assure you."

"And you will want to visit with your son, as well, I expect."

"Of course, of course. However, with such a charming young lady seeing to it that he is well entertained," the duke said, smiling in Lydia's direction, "I doubt he'll want my grizzled old visage in his sickroom."

Lydia smiled wanly in response to the compliment, but when Lady Smithfield cleared her throat, she hurried to remark, "I am pleased to be of assistance, Your Grace."

Emily thought her sister looked about as pleased as if she'd been told she was going to the guillotine, and wondered what she was portraying at the moment. Noble martyrdom, it appeared. Apparently Lydia felt there was no point in trying to resist their mother's efforts at matchmaking and was playing this new role to the hilt. Emily herself felt that neither she nor Lydia should be forced to marry Lord Wesleigh, but found herself more preoccupied with the mystery of Alexander Williams.

It was for that reason that she accompanied Lydia to Lord Wesleigh's chamber later that morning. Alexander had admitted to a close friendship with Lord Wesleigh in one of their earlier conversations; this was Emily's chance to discover more about the gentleman. Also, poor Lydia needed a chaperone, and moral support.

So it was Emily who tapped on Lord Wesleigh's door and opened it in response to his feeble, "Yes?"

"Good morning, Lord Wesleigh. Your father mentioned that you may be in need of a diversion, so Lydia and I have come to pay you a visit."

"My father mentioned that, did he?" Wesleigh drawled, and reached with one hand under the covers.

If he pulls out his quizzing glass I shall scream, Emily thought. Sure enough, the quizzing glass was found and retrieved.

"Well, come in, come in. Mustn't stand in the doorway. You are liable to create a draft. Drafts are very damaging to someone in my condition."

Emily walked calmly into the room, but Lydia eyed the man in the bed with trepidation and entered the room most reluctantly. "He is not going to eat you, you know," Emily whispered to her sister, who gave her a look of reproach and schooled her features into a travesty of a smile that Emily felt made her usually beautiful sister look downright ugly. The man in the bed apparently shared Emily's sentiments, for he dropped his quizzing glass abruptly and turned with a look of impatience toward Emily.

"How are you feeling today, Lord Wesleigh?" she

asked.

"Ghastly. I am sure I shan't be able to leave this chamber for a sennight, at least."

"Your father mentioned the same at breakfast this morning. Lydia thought to entertain you by reading to you. Would you enjoy that, Lord Wesleigh?" Emily thought to annoy him by speaking in the hearty tones of a governess to an unruly charge, and was rewarded by seeing his lips twitch into a semblance of a smile.

"I am not deaf, you know, just afflicted with a bad case of the grippe," he confided to her, neglecting to use the foppish drawl that had so annoyed her previously.

"I am relieved to discover you are neither deaf nor dumb, Lord Wesleigh," Emily replied, and smiled her first genuine smile at him.

The sight of that impish smile sent him reaching for his quizzing glass again, as if in protection, but before he was able to raise it to his face the young lady shocked him by removing it from his grasp.

"See here, Miss Smithfield—" he sputtered.

"I am sorry, my lord, but it is for your own good. I have just recently discovered that you are neither deaf nor dumb, and it is my suspicion you are not blind, either. However, if you persist in distorting your eyesight, you will find yourself wearing spectacles prematurely. I will just set your weapon, excuse me, quizzing glass, here on the table, where you can retrieve it when you are feeling more the thing."

"You, my girl, are a minx," he told her, looking much like a spoiled boy denied his favorite toy.

"And you, my lord, are a fraud. Now, I will leave Lydia here to read to you, and send Bess up to chaperone, as I feel I do not have the type of soothing presence that is desirable in a sickroom, as you would no doubt agree, my lord." She ignored the look of reproach from both parties in the room and slipped out. She would quiz Lord Wesleigh about his friend on another day. All of a sudden, her suspicions had seemed quite absurd. Such a foppish young man as Lord Wesleigh could not be the friend of a hardened criminal.

She peeked in the room an hour later to find Lydia gone and Lord Wesleigh in conversation with Alexander Williams.

"Oh, excuse me, I did not realize you had a guest." She turned to leave but was stopped by Williams, who had risen from his seat at her entrance.

"Please stay. We would welcome your company. Lord Wesleigh was just telling me how much he admires your sister." Alexander grinned down at Sir Marcus, who returned the look with a grimace. He had said nothing of the sort. In actuality, he had spent the ten minutes of Alexander's visit complaining about the girl.

"She reads with as much animation as a dashed corpse," he had told Alexander. "Which was bad enough, as I had the deuce of a time trying to stay awake, but, when I finally gave up the struggle and dozed off, I awoke to find her standing above me, her eyes welled up with tears. It was demmed embarrassing. I didn't know which way to look. 'Pon my word, Wesleigh, the girl walks around like a deuced martyr."

Alexander had laughed at the scene his friend had described, but he knew something had to be done about the situation. Apparently Lydia was as opposed to the match as he. The sooner this tangle was unraveled, the better.

At the moment, however, Emily was looking at him and his friend with suspicion writ large in her beautiful brown eyes. She had noticed the look they had exchanged and thought the gentlemen might be sharing a joke at her or her sister's expense. "My sister has many admirable qualities," she said, in response to Alexander's comment.

"She does, indeed." Alexander agreed. "However, I would much rather discuss *your* admirable qualities. I thought your performance on the pianoforte at dinner the other evening was very good, but what I just overheard was brilliant. Was that you playing just now?"

Emily looked embarrassed at his comment. "Yes, I was playing, and while I thank you for the compliment, it is undeserved. I practice too sporadically to be truly good. I find myself playing mostly when I want to work out something in my mind."

"Your thoughts must be quite tumultuous to inspire the performance I just heard. Perhaps it would help if you shared them."

Emily looked over at Lord Wesleigh, who was listening to her interchange with Williams with great interest. "I do not think so, Mr. Williams, but thank you for your concern."

"I am concerned. I want you to know that I will always stand your friend, Miss Smithfield," Alexander said, looking at her intently.

Emily was embarrassed by his look. It was obvious he was being sincere, but there seemed to be another message in the eyes that stared piercingly into hers. She felt very uncomfortable with Lord Wesleigh there.

"Thank you, Mr. Williams," she managed to reply, and then, in an attempt to lift the serious mood that had descended upon them, she said, "However, I fear Lord Wesleigh is not as kindly disposed toward me." She paused, and both Williams and Wesleigh looked at her in inquiry. "I stole his quizzing glass."

Alexander's lips twitched, but he remarked solemnly, "My dear girl, that is a heinous crime indeed."

Wesleigh roused himself to enter into the discussion. "Not a laughing matter, Alexander. The young lady forcibly removed my property."

"Poor chap," Alexander responded sympathetically, "I suppose you were unable to defend yourself in your weakened condition."

"Quite so," Wesleigh replied, his sullen, childish expression quite at odds with the elegance of his ruffled nightshirt and satin dressing gown. Emily's and Alexander's eyes met, and Emily had to bite her lip to keep from laughing.

It was probably fortunate that Bess arrived on the scene before Emily could wound Wesleigh's tender sensibilities any further. "Excuse me, miss, but Lady Abernathy and Lady Cynthia Sommers are downstairs and are wishing to see Lord Wesleigh."

Emily watched as Alexander and his friend exchanged a look, and wished she knew what they were thinking. It was obvious that Lady Cynthia's name had affected both of them in some manner. "Should I instruct Bess to bring the ladies up to your chamber, Lord Wesleigh?"

"No!" both men shouted in unison. Lord Wesleigh recovered himself first. "My dear girl," he said, affecting the foppish drawl that so annoyed Emily, "I am already feeling quite fatigued from the number of visitors I have entertained this morning. I could not possibly see anyone else in my weakened state."

"Of course not," Emily agreed. "We would not want you to suffer a relapse." Wesleigh looked at her with suspicion, but she returned the look with one of bland innocence. "Well, I suppose I should go downstairs and inform our guests you are not able to see them. I hope they are not too disappointed. Would you care to join me in the drawing room, Mr. Williams?"

"Um, no. No, thank you. I have a few more items to discuss with Wesleigh here."

Emily nodded and turned to leave. At the door she turned back. "You know, I just remarked upon the fact that you two have the same first name. Aren't you both named Alexander?"

Mr. Williams and Lord Wesleigh both looked blank for a moment, before Williams replied. "Yes, you are right. In fact it is a source of great amusement to our close friends. It can cause quite a bit of confusion in conversation." Williams managed a lame grin, and Wesleigh roused himself to smile as well.

"Quite a coincidence, what?" he asked. "Although I prefer Marcus, one of my second names, to Alexander. There's something quite supercilious-sounding about the name Alexander, don't you think?"

"Well, it is rather a mouthful, and it does put one in mind of a Greek conqueror," Emily replied, looking over the duo closely before again turning to leave. She wondered what it was about her innocent question that had produced such an odd reaction.

Eight

෨෮

Emily checked her appearance in the hallway mirror before proceeding into the drawing room. She was irritated with herself at the gesture, but she could not help herself. She found Lady Cynthia's cold perfection quite intimidating. Whatever confidence her reflection gave her was dispelled the moment she entered the drawing room. Lady Cynthia was quite the lady of fashion, in a sky-blue morning dress that matched her eyes perfectly. Well, perhaps not perfectly. Her eyes resembled ice more than they did sky.

"Good morning, Lady Abernathy, Lady Cynthia. How kind of you to call. Unfortunately, Lord Wesleigh does not feel well enough to receive visitors."

"Really. He told you so himself, I presume." Lady Cynthia replied.

"Yes, of course. He asked me to convey his regrets, but he feared a relapse of his illness were he to entertain visitors."

"And he told you this while you were *visiting* him?" Lady Cynthia met Emily's glance with a limpid stare.

"It was a brief visit, I assure you. There was not enough time for me to compromise him, or for him to propose marriage, if that is what you fear." Emily realized her remark was rather shocking, but she was beyond caring. What could Lady Cynthia do to her? She had forgotten Lady Abernathy's presence.

"Well!" that august lady proclaimed in loud accents, looking down her long nose at Emily.

"I apologize, Lady Abernathy. I must have misunderstood Lady Cynthia's concern. I am sure her interest in Lord Wesleigh's well-being is the same as it would be for any unfortunate victim of the grippe, and is not reserved for wealthy heirs to a dukedom."

As the apology was as offensive to Lady Cynthia as Emily's initial remark, it was not to be expected that Lady Cynthia's anger was assuaged by this reply. However, as she felt Emily was entirely beneath her notice and not attractive enough to be a serious rival, she merely smiled a superior smile, and replied, "Just so."

There was a definite chill in the air as Lady Smithfield and Lydia entered the room. They greeted their guests graciously and apologized for their delay in joining them. "But I am sure Emily and Lady Cynthia took advantage of this opportunity to get to know one another better," Lady Smithfield remarked, oblivious to the tension in the room.

Emily reflected that her mother was right; she had gotten to know Lady Cynthia better. She was a materialistic, scheming snob, determined to entrap Lord Wesleigh into marriage. Emily conveniently forgot that she herself had had such an ambition only a few days previously. Now she had no interest in the marquess beyond that of a guest in her home. However, as much as his dandified ways annoyed her, he did not deserve such a wife as Lady Cynthia.

Lady Smithfield and Lady Abernathy assumed the

burden of the conversation, but it was soon clear that they were to get on no better than Emily and Lady Cynthia.

"My dear Lady Abernathy, you have heard, of course, that we have two distinguished guests at the moment."

Lady Abernathy regally inclined her head. Lady Smithfield was not dissuaded by her visitor's lack of enthusiasm.

"The duke of Alford, and his son, Lord Wesleigh. The duchess and I were at school together you know." Lady Abernathy gave a second nod, an almost imperceptible move of her head. "Lady Abernathy, as we are such good friends, perhaps I can share something with you. In strictest confidence, of course." Lady Abernathy's nod was a little more vigorous, and she allowed a slight gleam of interest to appear on her craggy countenance.

Lydia and Emily exchanged horrified glances. "Mama," Emily ventured, in a voice of warning.

"It is all right, Emily. I was just going to tell Lady Abernathy of the duchess's wish, and mine, that Lydia and Lord Wesleigh marry. That is no secret, in any case."

"Hmmph." In a less refined lady, what Lady Abernathy did might be termed a snort. "I feel I should warn you that you are destined for disappointment."

Lady Smithfield's pleasant expression slipped just a little. "I am sure I do not know what you mean, Lady Abernathy. Why do you feel I will experience disappointment?"

"Because Lord Wesleigh has been paying very marked attentions to my niece, Lady Cynthia." Lady

Abernathy turned to Cynthia for confirmation, and it was Lady Cynthia's turn to give an imperceptible nod of her head.

"Of course, one does not brag of one's conquests," Lady Cynthia began with a little trill of laughter.

"Then why is she doing so?" Emily whispered to Lydia.

"But, I must admit," Lady Cynthia resumed, with a glare at Emily, "that before Lord Wesleigh left London, all of London society was in daily anticipation of a notice in the *Morning Post.*"

"Really? Had they lost something?" Emily asked, in feigned innocence.

"Of course not. They were in anticipation of a notice of Lord Wesleigh's betrothal to myself." Lady Cynthia lowered her eyes in a well-simulated display of maidenly modesty. "I am sure it was immodest of me to admit to such a thing. Pray do not discuss it with anyone."

"Well, if all of London is speaking of it, I do not see what good it would do for us to hold our tongues." Emily spoke ostensibly to Lydia, but in a voice loud enough to be overheard by all the inhabitants of the small drawing room.

Before Lady Cynthia could devise some cutting remark, Lady Smithfield had arisen from her seat, and to Lady Cynthia's dismay, had crossed to her side to sit beside her. "My poor, dear child," she said, taking one of Lady Cynthia's hands in her own, "I hope your feelings are not deeply engaged."

Before Lady Cynthia could respond, Lady Abernathy entered the conversation. "Really, Elizabeth, what a vulgar remark."

Lady Smithfield turned in surprise to Lady Aber-nathy. "But, Mildred, surely it is obvious what is hap-pening here. Lord Wesleigh has been trifling with the affections of your poor niece." She turned back to Lady Cynthia. "I am sorry, my dear, to mention it so abruptly, but that is why I inquired first as to whether your feel-ings were seriously engaged."

"Madam," Lady Cynthia replied, wrestling her hand from Lady Smithfield's grasp, "I fear you are mistaken."

"Oh, no," Lady Smithfield said, still looking at Lady Cynthia with sympathy, "you see, the duke and his son are visiting us with the purpose of making an alliance with *our* family."

Emily, who had realized that her mother had reached the limit of her endurance, was not surprised by the an-nouncement. Lydia did not appear surprised, either. As she was wont to walk about in a state of continual de-spair for the past week, her countenance did not change noticeably.

The same could not be said of Lady Abernathy and Lady Cynthia, who both had similar expressions on their aristocratic faces. It was quite enlightening to Emily, who felt she was getting a glimpse of what Lady Cynthia would look like in forty years. More than ever did she pity the poor man who would tie himself to Lady Cyn-thia.

"How absurd!" Lady Abernathy stated, the first to regain her composure. "You have misunderstood the situation, I am sure."

Lady Smithfield drew herself up in affront. "Are you implying that I am a liar, Lady Abernathy?"

"Of course not. Merely confused."

"I am not confused. I had a letter from the duke, spelling out his intentions in detail. A notice is to appear in the *Morning Post* at the end of the month."

Lady Abernathy was stricken speechless for the first time in her life. Lady Smithfield observed the stunned inhabitants of her drawing room and almost began to enjoy the situation.

Emily felt a little of her mother's vindication as well. Forgetting for the moment that she had no desire for her or her sister to wed the marquess, she gloried in seeing the crack in Lady Cynthia's haughty veneer. Emily did not believe for a moment that Lady Cynthia had any tender feelings for the marquess, so she did not believe the news could do her any lasting harm.

All were surprised when Lydia spoke. "Perhaps, Mama, if Lady Cynthia has a prior claim to the marquess's affections . . ." She faltered under her mother's severe gaze.

"Nonsense. It is obvious he was not serious in his intentions."

Lady Cynthia's alabaster complexion turned red. "I do not believe you can speak with such authority on the matter, Lady Smithfield."

"My dear girl, although I did not witness the marquess's attentions to you, I can tell you with authority that it is quite common for an idle gentleman to enjoy a flirtation with a pretty girl such as yourself."

Lady Cynthia did not know whether to be more insulted that her charms, commonly described as beautiful and incomparable, were relegated to a mere "pretty," or the implication that she had been a momentary diversion for a bored nobleman. She rose in a huff and turned to her aunt. "Aunt Mildred, I refuse to stay in this house a minute longer."

"Of course, Cynthia. We shall leave at once. Lady Smithfield, Miss Smithfield, Miss Emily Smithfield," Lady Abernathy addressed her hostess and her daughters, "I can only say that I am very disappointed, and I shall not bid you a good day."

"Well! That was most unpleasant," Lady Smithfield stated, a frown on her face. She turned to her daughters to find Emily stifling a giggle. "Emily, child, what is there to smile about?"

"I am sorry, Mama, but the look on Lady Cynthia's face . . ." She could hold her laughter back no longer, and it was only a few seconds before her mother joined in. Even Lydia could not maintain her tragic mood in the face of her mother and sister's hilarity, and was soon giggling as well.

When the laughter subsided, Lady Smithfield grew sober once more. "I only hope Lady Abernathy sends us an invitation to her ball after this episode."

"Oh, Mama, do you think she would not?" Emily grew sober as well. She was looking forward to the ball.

Lady Abernathy considered for a moment. Then a wide smile appeared on her face. "No, I do not. After all, she could hardly invite our guests were she to exclude us."

She started laughing again, and after a moment or two, so did Emily and Lydia.

৪০০৪

Emily still had a smile on her face when she knocked on Lord Wesleigh's door a few minutes later.

"Come."

Emily opened the door but stayed in the doorway. "I just wanted to tell you that our guests have left, and they send you their regards." Emily could not remember if they had done so or not, but figured they probably would have if they were not in such a hurry to get out of the house. The thought made her grin.

Alexander and Marcus looked at her in suspicion. Alexander had been afraid to leave until after Lady Cynthia and her aunt were long gone, as he had not wanted to run the risk of meeting them, so he was still in his friend's chamber.

"You appear as if you found their visit pleasant," Alexander ventured.

"Oh, indeed. *I* enjoyed it tremendously."

Alexander and Marcus exchanged a look. "Really. I did not realize Lady Cynthia was of such a congenial disposition. Perhaps I was mistaken in her," Marcus said. This innocent comment had Emily grinning even wider.

"Tsk, tsk. You should not speak so disparagingly of your inamorata. She had much kinder things to say about you."

"My what!" Marcus exclaimed, before Alexander nudged him in the shoulder. He had forgotten for the moment that he was not himself, but Wesleigh. And there had been rumors of his friend's involvement with the girl.

Emily felt that such a discussion should not be carried on in the hallway. So she proceeded a few more feet into the room. "I am sorry," she said, with a look of wide-eyed innocence. "Is that not the appropriate word for it? I did not mean to imply the relationship was not all that it should be."

Marcus looked at Alexander in irritation. "You and your intrigues," he muttered, only loud enough for Alexander to hear. Then he tried to think what Alexander would say if in this situation. "My dear girl, you must realize that my involvement with Lady Cynthia was not of a serious nature," he told Emily. "It was just a light-hearted flirtation. I realize that you are not familiar with the ways of London society, but that sort of thing happens all the time."

"That is just what Mama told her," she assured Marcus, still the picture of innocence, but the barely suppressed smile giving her away.

"Your mother told Lady Cynthia what?" Alexander exclaimed, his look of amusement fading.

"Let me see . . ." Emily paused as if struggling to remember. "I believe she said that 'idle gentleman often amuse themselves by flirting with pretty girls.' That was, of course, in response to Lady Cynthia's disclosure that she and Lord Wesleigh were engaged."

"What!" Both men exclaimed in unison. Emily was enjoying herself immensely.

"Oh, I beg your pardon, she did not come out and say you were engaged," she assured Marcus. "She just said that the announcement of your betrothal was expected at any moment. Dear me, I suppose I should not have repeated that. She did ask us to keep her confidence. However, I did not suppose there would be any harm in telling you. After all, I assume you would already be aware of the engagement if it were due to be announced at any moment."

Marcus looked rather helplessly at his friend. Alexander nobly rose to the occasion, though he was reeling at the disclosure. How dared Lady Cynthia tell people they were engaged! He should have known better than to say two words to her, let alone flirt with her. "Miss Smithfield, I am sure you realize that a man in a position like Wesleigh here is liable to receive unwanted attention from females."

Emily turned her innocent gaze in Alexander's direction. "Then he did not flirt with her?"

Little minx, Alexander thought. *Laughing at us all behind that wide-eyed look.* "Well, he may have flirted with her, but I can assure you, he had no intention of marrying her."

"Quite right," Marcus agreed, seeing a vision of himself forced to marry Lady Cynthia while masquerading as Lord Wesleigh flash before his eyes. "The girl has a vivid imagination."

"Well, I can only say that I am sure Mama will be relieved to hear that." She turned to leave the room, pausing before closing the door to remark, "Because she told Lady Abernathy and Lady Cynthia that you purposed to make an alliance with *our* family." She shut the door quickly, but not before the gentlemen heard her giggle at the sight of Marcus's dismayed expression.

"What a saucy girl it is," Marcus said, shaking his head in disbelief. "Are you certain you want her? She will be a rare handful."

"Oh, I am certain. She is exactly what I need. I cannot envision a dull moment with Emily around." Alexander began to smile. "I must admit I would have liked to have been there when Lady Smithfield told the so-proper Lady Cynthia that she had been no more than a trifling flirtation."

"I cannot imagine how you struck up a flirtation with the girl in the first place," Marcus said in disgust. "I would think you would have had better luck coaxing a kiss from a stone."

"But that was exactly it. It was the challenge of the thing. She was an ice princess, and I had visions of heating her up a bit. I realized my folly pretty soon, let me tell you, and I spent most of our so-called flirtation running away from her as fast as I could. I guess I should thank my father, or I could have ended up married to the girl.

"Enough talk of Lady Cynthia. How is the pursuit of our spy coming?" Alexander asked Marcus.

"I scouted around last night looking for his hideout, and I cannot find a likely spot."

"Perhaps he lives underground, like a mole," Alexander suggested, joking.

"That is not as absurd a statement as you might think," Marcus told him. "You have heard of the Hawkhurst Gang, I presume?"

"Yes, they were quite notorious. I forgot that they were from this part of the country. But they are all long dead. What have they to do with our highwayman?"

"It is said they had underground tunnels from Hawkhurst to Stonehurst and beyond. Perhaps our highwayman is using the tunnels to escape detection."

"That is an interesting premise. Have you located any of these tunnels?"

"I have heard that one of the tunnels originates from the Tudor Arms. I am to pay a visit to the place this evening and see what I can find."

"Would you appreciate some company?" Alexander asked.

"I am not sure you have the talent for acting that I have." Sir Marcus grinned, slipping back into his foppish role. "My grandmother was an actress, don't you know."

"I seem to remember you saying as much," Alexander replied. "Still, you are liable to ruin your jacket in such a seedy place. Or someone could take exception to your golden locks."

"You may come if you wish. However, I could definitely use some help on Saturday night. There is a courier traveling with a missive from Whitehall. It would be a logical time for our man to strike."

"I would be happy to help you apprehend the traitor. In fact, I wouldn't dream of missing it."

Nine

এ৫৩

Emily knocked gently on Lord Wesleigh's door, not wanting to disturb him if he was sleeping. Apparently he was not. There was a shuffling sound and a thump.

"Lord Wesleigh? Are you all right?" Emily asked from the other side of the door.

"Fine, fine. Just dropped my book. Give me a moment." Marcus scrambled to get back into the bed and under the covers.

Emily patiently waited a few minutes before heeding Marcus's call to come in.

"I am sorry to disturb you, my lord. I just wanted to check in on you. Do you need anything?"

"No, no, I am fine," Marcus assured her.

"You look rather flushed," Emily said, peering at Wesleigh speculatively. She wondered how sick Lord Wesleigh really was. Perhaps this was all an elaborate ploy to avoid social doings with her family. She grew angry at the notion this fop thought he was better than she or Lydia, conveniently forgetting that she and her sister had rejected him first. Irritated by her suspicions, she regretted the sympathetic impulse that had prompted her to check on him.

"Just the fever, I expect," he replied, coughing unconvincingly into his handkerchief.

Emily nodded and turned to leave.

"You are not going?" Marcus asked plaintively.

"Why, yes. I just stopped in for a moment."

"But, I am bored to flinders. Stay for a while. Please."

Emily smiled, her temper restored. Oh, well. She supposed it would not hurt to entertain him for a while. It was the polite thing to do. He was a guest in their home, after all. "All right, I will stay. What would you like to do?"

"I don't know. A game of chess, perhaps?"

Emily nodded agreeably, although she was rather bored with chess. The duke of Alford was a devotee of the game, and she had spent the last two evenings playing him after dinner. She retrieved the chess set anyway and set it up on the table beside the bed. They played a rather desultory game, which Emily won easily. As she was putting the game away, she asked Marcus about his friend.

"Mr. Williams tells me you two have known each other a long time."

"What? Oh, yes. We are rather close. We see a lot of each other in London."

"Oh? Does Mr. Williams travel to London often? I would have suspected his duties as curate keep him quite occupied."

"Quite so. He doesn't get to London as often as he would like, but comes whenever he can get away for a time. Which is not often enough, in my opinion. I cannot abide the country. The society is so limited, and there are few decent occupations to be found." Marcus began fiddling with his quizzing glass, apparently unaware that he had just insulted his hostess. Emily just smiled to herself, having learned not to take Lord Wesleigh too seriously.

"I don't recall ever having met you in London, Miss Smithfield," Marcus said, thinking that it was a good thing he had not.

"No, we do not travel to London much." Emily sighed. "My father used to take me occasionally when he was alive, but I have not been in nearly five years."

"Pity. I could see you fitting in rather well in London."

"Really?"

"Oh, yes. You would be a refreshing change to the simpering girls that one meets. I think you would make quite a splash."

"Oh, I do not think so, but I appreciate the compliment. My ambitions are modest. I have no desire to make a splash, just meet some new people."

"Well, London's the place to do so," Marcus assured her. "Particularly during the season. More people than you can shake a stick at."

Emily almost mentioned she did not think one should shake sticks at people, but did not think Lord Wesleigh would appreciate her attempt at humor. Instead, she said, rather wistfully, "Well, it is no use speculating about it, because it's unlikely I'll ever be in London for the season." Emily determinedly changed the subject, and they discussed music for a while. During the course of the conversation, they agreed to dispense with the formalities and were soon calling each other by their first names. Of course, as Marcus did not wish to be called Alexander, Emily agreed to call him by his preferred name, Marcus. She discovered she knew some of his favorite pieces, and offered to play for him. Marcus agreed enthusiastically, as he thought he would lose his mind if he had to look at the same four walls any longer. He told her he thought he could manage to walk down the stairs to the drawing room.

"Oh, no, my lord, I mean, Marcus. You mustn't risk your health in that manner. You can hear the music very well from here, as I will be sure to leave the door to your chamber open." Emily still suspected his illness might only be a pretense, and could not resist punishing him a little.

"Very well," he said, a little sulkily.

Emily hid her smile and went to play the pianoforte, as promised. She had been playing for about half an hour when Alexander arrived to visit his friend. He found Marcus sitting upright in bed, eyes closed, and a smile on his face.

"I hope I am not interrupting anything," Alexander said from the doorway, an ironic smile on his face.

"Alex. You startled me. No, dashed glad to see you, actually. A chap gets bored sitting in bed all day."

"You do not look bored at the moment, however."

"No. I have been enjoying the music." He made a motion in the air in the direction of the drawing room. "Emily has been playing some of my favorite songs."

"Emily, is it?" Alexander asked.

"She asked me to call her that when I insisted she call me Marcus. To tell you the truth, I was sick to death of having to answer to your name. There's nothing improper in it," Marcus insisted, when Alexander continued to stare suspiciously at him.

"I am sure there is not. Did she know they were your favorites or was it just a fortunate guess on her part?"

"No, I told her. She has been very accommodating this morning. She's a very nice girl, Emily Smithfield. I can see why you admire her."

"Indeed," Alexander agreed, but his eyes narrowed suspiciously. "She spent some time with you this morning?"

"Yes, I told her she ought to go to London. 'Tis rather a shame she has to be stuck in the country like this. When I think of what a good modiste could accomplish . . ." Sir Marcus's voice trailed off, as he became lost envisioning playing Pygmalion to Emily's Galatea. He shook himself from his reverie, and continued, "Regardless, we both agreed she would benefit from a broader circle of friends she could make in London society. She finds the country somewhat confining."

"Apparently the country is not too confining. She seems to have made one new friend already."

Marcus smiled. "Well, I hope so. One can never have too many friends."

"Particularly when the friend is an attractive young lady who believes you to be the heir to a dukedom."

Marcus's smile faded. "I do not think I appreciate your remark, or your tone of voice. If you are trying to make some sort of implication, I can only say you're far off the mark. I do not have any designs on your lady, nor does she on me."

"Well, I believe that you may not be interested in her, I know you don't have any wish to be leg-shackled, but you must remember that Emily believes you to be highly eligible."

"I think you are doing her a disservice. Her attentions to me have been those of a gracious hostess to a guest in her home, and nothing more."

Alexander shook his head, a skeptical look on his face. "Here speaks the man who has not been the target of grasping females for the past ten years."

"I tell you, Alex, I think all the attention has spoiled you for a good female. You cannot believe there are any decent women out there who would be interested in a gentleman for anything other than his title and fortune. For your information, Emily tried to lead the conversation to a discussion of you, but I had no desire to contradict whatever you may have told her concerning your assumed identity, and turned the subject."

Alexander relaxed a little and looked at his friend hopefully. "She asked about me, did she?"

"Yes, she did. Although I am starting to think you don't deserve a nice girl like Emily. Lady Cynthia might be the better match for you after all."

Sir Marcus was prevented from saying anything else by the pillow his best friend smashed into his face.

෨෬

Emily and Lydia made a trip to the vicarage early Friday morning to deliver some sewing they had done for a few of the poorer families in the parish. Emily viewed this as a perfect opportunity for Lydia and Sedgewick to spend some time alone with each other. She had been distracted from her original intention to get them together by the visit of the duke and his son, but she had not lost sight of her goal.

She thought it was a little too bad that neither she

nor Lydia could love Lord Wesleigh, for if one had to marry, she supposed it would be preferable to marry someone with money. She had formed a better opinion of Lord Wesleigh over the past few days, but she still knew she did not feel for him what one should feel for one's husband. She supposed she would have to resign herself to life as a spinster, but she felt that Lydia, at least, should have her chance at happiness.

Lydia was absorbed in her own thoughts, as well, so the walk to the vicarage was accomplished in near silence. They were admitted into a comfortable room set up as a library by Mrs. Baker, Sedgewick's housekeeper. Emily had been inside the vicarage before, but now that she knew her sister was interested in Sedgewick, she was far more interested in her surroundings. Yes, it was quite cozy, and she believed her sister would be very comfortable there. Emily wondered if she herself could be comfortable in a country vicarage such as this, and felt that she could, with the right vicar. She shook her head, as if to dispel such a thought. The curate she was fantasizing about would probably never see the inside of another vicarage. He was more likely to see the inside of Newgate.

Her thoughts were interrupted by the entrance of Sedgewick and Williams. Emily explained the purpose of their visit, and Sedgewick thanked them for their charity in bringing the linens.

"Would you like some refreshments? Some tea, perhaps?" Sedgewick offered.

Before Lydia had a chance to refuse, Emily took a seat, mentioning that would be quite the thing. As Jonathan asked Mrs. Baker to bring the tea tray, Emily thought furiously for an excuse to leave Sedgewick and Lydia alone together.

"Mr. Williams, Lord Wesleigh asked me to relay a message to you," Emily began.

"Yes?" Alexander responded.

"Well, actually, it was more something he wanted me to show you."

"Really," Alexander replied, "How peculiar."

Emily swallowed bravely, and continued. "Yes, he was quite sure you would appreciate the daffodils growing in the graveyard. He noticed them when he passed the church on his way to Smithfield House, and he thought you would appreciate the sight."

"And so I would." Alexander was beginning to realize what Emily was attempting to do, although he felt her pretext for leaving the two alone was rather a poor one.

"Perhaps we could go look at them now."

"The very thing," Alexander agreed.

Emily and Alexander rose to leave the room, but Lydia protested. "Emily, I am sure Mr. Williams can look at them at his leisure. The church is not so close as you might think."

"Nonsense, it is not that great a distance. And Lord Wesleigh told me particularly to observe Mr. Williams's reaction and report it back to him. Apparently he and Mr. Williams are staunch admirers of Mr. Wordsworth, and the sight of the 'host of golden daffodils' in the graveyard put Lord Wesleigh in mind of Wordsworth's poem, 'I Wandered Lonely As a Cloud.'"

Lydia and Sedgewick were looking at Emily as though she had sprouted another head, but she hurried from the room with Williams before they could protest further.

"So where is this 'host of daffodils'?" Alexander asked Emily as they walked toward the graveyard.

"I am not sure there are any. It is now the end of May, and I believe they begin blooming in March. We had better begin looking for some, however, in case Sedgewick or Lydia asks us when we return. I think they are already questioning my veracity, if not my sanity."

"Well, I must admit that your excuse was rather uninspired."

"Contrary to what you may believe, I do not have much practice in the art of deception and intrigue. And I also had very little cooperation. You would almost think they do not want to be alone together."

"Yes," Alexander agreed, "it is quite unnatural for two people supposedly in love to have such an aversion to each other's company. I, on the other hand, am quite appreciative of my good fortune."

Emily was embarrassed by the remark, as she could not miss its implication, and tried to change the subject. "Well, whatever you may think of my excuse, I thought the Wordsworth bit was quite good."

Although Alexander might find fault with the excuse itself, he could not fault its results. It was a beautiful, sunny day, with only a light breeze, and he was entirely at peace with himself and the world. Emily made a charming picture in her sprigged muslin dress and gypsy bonnet, and, though they saw no daffodils, there were alyssum, columbine, and hyacinth in abundance. It appeared, in fact, as if all of Kent was in bloom, and, although nothing was more natural than for flowers to bloom in the springtime, especially in a part of the country known as the Garden of England, at that moment Alexander felt it as a particular compliment to himself and the lady.

The church itself was situated in a pleasant aspect, it being nearly the highest point in the parish; the village, with its charming half-timbered houses and shops, was spread out below them. Alexander thought himself at the top of the world, and it was obvious that Emily shared his delight in the day and company.

They finally reached the graveyard and began wandering rather aimlessly among the headstones. They paused here and there to read an epitaph, but there was no morbid sense of death and depression. Alexander picked some daisies and presented them to Emily with a flourish, and she thanked him prettily, but promised to leave them at the grave of a Mary Simpson, whose epitaph they had just read, before they left the graveyard. In her present guise, Alexander thought her the quintessential country maiden and could not picture her hobnobbing with the bored and sated nobility in London. But perhaps he was mistaken in thinking that light in her eyes would ever be extinguished by *ennui*. Alexander stopped walking, and Emily turned to face him, still grasping her daisies. They had continued discussing poetry after Emily's mention of Wordsworth, and, after a long pause, while the air around them seemed to crackle with tension, Alexander resumed the conversation. "I prefer one of Wordsworth's other poems: 'She Was a Phantom of Delight.' Are you familiar with that one?" he asked.

His voice had grown softer, and there was a tender

look in his eyes as he regarded her. Emily could only nod, her breath caught in her throat. He began to recite softly,

"She was a Phantom of delight
When first she gleamed upon my sight;
A lovely Apparition, sent
To be a moment's ornament;
Her eyes as stars of Twilight fair;
Like Twilight's, too, her dusky hair;
But all things else about her drawn
From May-time and the cheerful Dawn;
A dancing Shape, an Image gay,
To haunt, to startle, and way-lay."

He paused, and drew her gently into his arms, leaning closer and closer until he was just a breath away from her lips. "'A perfect Woman, nobly planned, to warn, to comfort, and command,'" he finished, the last word barely distinguishable as their lips met.

Emily could no more resist his kiss than she could fly to the moon. His words had turned her insides to mush, and she felt herself returning his kiss with a passion she did not know she possessed. Time was suspended, and nothing else existed except her and Alexander. The moment was over far too soon, and Alexander raised his head, still holding Emily in his arms.

"Obviously you are not an admirer of Marvell," she said, when she could speak again. Even then she did not recognize her own voice.

Alexander could only look at her in confusion. Whatever reaction he had expected, it was not this. "What?" he asked.

"'The grave's a fine and private place, But none, I

think, do there embrace,'" Emily recited.

Alexander laughed. "I do not think that is a proper poem for you to know, my girl." He lowered his head as if to kiss her again, but she evaded him. "Someone might see us," she protested.

"You are right. Marvell was wrong about graveyards. This is far too public a place to share an embrace. I seem to lose my head whenever I am with you," he said, reaching for her hand instead and placing a kiss inside her palm. He closed her fingers over the kiss.

"We should probably return to the vicarage," Emily suggested shyly, afraid to meet his eyes. She was quite embarrassed at her lack of decorum, and was even more humiliated to discover the daisies she had been holding were scattered about their feet, apparently dropped by her during their embrace, though she had no recollection of it.

Alexander nodded, gave her his arm, and they turned to walk back. "I can only hope that Sedgewick and Lydia have used their time alone to such advantage," he said, smiling at the thought.

Try as she might, Emily could not imagine the so-proper Lydia and Sedgewick exchanging the searing kiss she and Alexander had just shared. *Perhaps there is something to be said for propriety,* Emily thought, as she realized she might live to regret her actions if Alexander were really the fiend she suspected he was.

ೞ

After Emily and Williams left, Lydia and Sedgewick were left looking at each other in uncomfortable silence.

"I must apologize for my sister's behavior, Mr.

Sedgewick," Lydia offered, looking up at Sedgewick through her eyelashes.

"Think nothing of it, Miss Smithfield. Your sister's behavior could never influence my respect and esteem for you," Mr. Sedgewick replied formally.

"Thank you, sir. The knowledge that you respect and esteem me is more comforting than you can ever know." She was the picture of despair, her head bowed, her eyes downcast. She could not help but raise them for one quick peek at Sedgewick, to see what effect her pose was having on him.

It was having all the effect she could have desired. "My dear Miss Smithfield, it pains me deeply to see you in such distress. I would do anything to alleviate your sorrow," Sedgewick told her, crossing the room to sit beside her on the settee.

"Alas," Lydia said, raising her eyes at last to his, "I fear there is nothing that can be done."

"But, please, tell me, what has caused you such distress?"

"Mr. Sedgewick, I do not think you can be entirely unaware of the plans my mother has conceived for me."

"No, Miss Smithfield, I am not ignorant of them." Sedgewick said. "She intends for you to marry, I believe."

"She does, indeed, sir. To a gentleman with whom I am not even acquainted." She looked up again, tears forming in her big blue eyes. "I must admit I have no desire for this marriage to take place. Yet I do not want to be disobedient to my mother's wishes."

"Of course you do not. I have often admired your strength of character, your moral integrity and virtue.

You do not esteem lightly the dictates of family and conscience. It is your sense of duty and moral rectitude that makes you so appealing to one, such as I, who regards a woman's character more than her outward appearance."

If Lydia found this compliment lacking in any way, it was not apparent. She blushed fiercely, but still managed to smile at the young gentleman who, whatever he might say to the contrary, was regarding her outward appearance with every semblance of delight. The slight smile gave Sedgewick the courage to reach for her hand. "Miss Smithfield, I have no right to speak what is in my heart." Lydia did not know how to react to this promising statement, so she only nodded, and did not try to remove her hand from his grasp. "So I will not," Sedgewick continued. Lydia tried her best to conceal her disappointment. "Neither can I encourage a daughter to act in opposition to her mother's wishes." At this speech, Lydia removed her hand. "However, although I do not counsel you to oppose your mother, I think it only right that you should be honest with her as to your feelings."

"What do you think I should do?" Lydia asked.

"It is not my place to tell you what to do."

Lydia masterfully concealed her impatience at this remark, and Sedgewick continued. "But it is my feeling that a loving mother, such as I am convinced Lady Smithfield is, would be desirous of knowing your true feelings regarding the proposed match. And, as a loving mother, she could hardly force you into a position that you would find repugnant."

This was not the answer Lydia wanted, and it seemed a shame that a scene that had such a promising beginning had gone so awry. "But, as you know, it is the desire of every mother to see her daughter successfully wed. She may not agree to the dissolution of her previous plan if it is unlikely that I will marry anyone else." Modesty forbade Lydia from making her point any clearer.

Sedgewick reached for her hand again. "Miss Smithfield, such a prospect is entirely unlikely, even absurd. Your mother will realize that there are many gentlemen who would count it a great honor indeed to marry her beautiful daughter. No, I am convinced that if you are honest with your mother about your feelings, you will prevail."

Lydia nodded in response, but wondered why, if so many gentlemen would count it an honor to marry her, the dolt sitting beside her would not make a positive effort in that direction.

៛០៰

Emily and Alexander entertained sentiments similar to Lydia's when they returned to the vicarage to find Lydia and Sedgewick sipping tea with expressions of noble resignation on their faces and in no greater charity with each other than they were before they had been left alone. It then began to occur to Emily that Sedgewick was as fond of melodrama as her sister. Emily believed that he harbored genuine feelings for Lydia, and Alexander had confirmed that belief, so his hesitance in declaring himself did not seem to spring from lack of affection. Indeed, Emily had observed him closely over tea, and his eyes appeared to follow Lydia's every move, in such a way as to confirm his regard. Yet, when it would become obvious to him that he was regarding Lydia tenderly, his entire countenance would change, and he would steadfastly refuse to peer in Lydia's direction for an extended time, until once again his feelings would overcome his resolution, and he would begin peeping in her direction once again.

Lydia herself added nothing to the occasion, as she had resumed her tragic role and was playing it to the hilt, with frequent glances in Sedgewick's direction to see how he responded to the airs she had assumed. Emily and Alexander watched the two of them with much amusement, but then became so involved in their own conversation that they were able to forget that Lydia and Sedgewick were present, for the most part. Emily was doing her best to forget a great many things; that Alexander was a penniless curate, for one, and that she had just allowed a gentleman whom she had no intention of marrying and suspected of being a highwayman to embrace her in a graveyard, of all places. She resolutely put those thoughts from her mind and determined to enjoy this one last glorious afternoon in his company, and even Lydia's sighs and Sedgewick's disapproving glances could not weigh on her high spirits, which had an almost frenzied quality about them.

Alexander himself could not remember ever having spent a more glorious afternoon, and resolved to put an end to this charade by declaring himself at the earliest opportunity, unaware of the doubts that plagued his beloved.

It was with regret that Emily announced that they must return home. Lydia was by this time in such a morose state that she was barely cognizant of her surroundings. She awoke to them with a start, agreeing that their visit had been much too long and that their mother would be concerned about them if they did not return with all possible haste.

Lydia was correct in her assumption that their mother was concerned about them. However, it was not fears for her daughters' safety that troubled Lady Smithfield. She was highly disturbed that her two girls had spent an entire afternoon, most of the day, really, in company with a vicar and a curate, when a highly eligible marquess lay languishing in his chamber. Although not the most observant of women generally speaking, she had noted Lydia's lack of enthusiasm for Lord Wesleigh's company and was dismayed by what she had observed. Her previous conjectures about the match had been as romantic as Emily's. Lydia and Lord Wesleigh were to fit into their parents' plans for them by falling in love at their first meeting. After all, a rich young lord was the embodiment of a girl's dreams. How could he be other than handsome and charming?

She had been a little stymied by the actual appearance of Lord Wesleigh, but only for a moment. He was given a little too much to matters of dress, but while Lydia and Emily saw a fop, Lady Smithfield, in all her romanticism, saw a man quite distinguished by his attire, one who would always stand out in a crowd, a peacock among vultures. His being ill, too, while at first thought of as an impediment to the progress of his relationship with Lydia, was soon romanticized as well. In many cases love was kindled by sympathy, and Lydia, in particular, was the most sympathetic of young ladies. She could not help but commiserate with Lord Wesleigh in his sickness, and such a tender feeling was bound to lead to one even more tender. And, with Lord Wesleigh confined to his chamber, he and Lydia had the opportunity of spending hours in close association, quite removed from any other society.

With such reasoning as this did Lady Smithfield dismiss any misgivings she might have about arbitrarily arranging the lives of two young people without consulting them on the matter. She had noticed, however, that things were not falling out exactly as she had arranged them in her mind. When peeking into Lord Wesleigh's room on occasion, expecting to find Lydia in conversation with the invalid, Emily would be there in her stead, with Lydia nowhere to be found. And Lydia's depression of spirits was quite noticeable as well. Lady Smithfield had always been pleased with Lydia's calm demeanor, valuing it more than Emily's vivacious manner, which in her opinion, bordered on the impertinent. Yet there was no denying that a little more liveliness in Lydia's behavior would not be amiss. Since the marquess's arrival, Lydia had walked about looking like a ghost.

It was in this state of mind that Lady Smithfield waited with impatience for her daughters to return home. When they finally did arrive, she said nothing of the length of time they had been gone but asked instead after Mr. Sedgewick's health and that of his guest. She knew that she had been right to worry when both her daughters' cheeks grew rosy at such an innocent question, and they began to pay far too much attention to the removal of their bonnets and smoothing out any wrinkles in their dresses. She was too wise to comment on their discomposure, or quiz Lydia on her feelings for Lord Wesleigh at present. Although Lydia was the most dutiful of daughters, there was no denying that she was also highly imaginative. If she fancied herself in love with the vicar, as Lady Smithfield was beginning to suspect, opposition from her mother might fix her affection irrevocably on Jonathan Sedgewick. So she avoided the subject of gentlemen altogether, initiating a discussion instead on what they were to wear to the Abernathy's ball Wednesday the following week, an invitation to which had finally arrived.

Ten
ಬಿಂಬ

Lady Smithfield remained in the drawing room with the duke after her daughters had retired for the evening. She wished to discuss with him her suspicion that the match between their children was not proceeding as planned. He listened quite attentively to her fears and commended her for her wisdom in saying nothing to Lydia about Jonathan Sedgewick. But he assured her that his son was quite enamored of her daughter.

"Really?" Lady Smithfield asked in relieved surprise. "He told you so?"

"In explicit language. He admires your daughter tremendously, and nothing would bring him greater joy than to marry her, but he is concerned that she may not return his regard. So he is wooing her, in his own way. But you know these young people today. He insists on doing things completely on his own, with no interference from you or me. I agreed to leave the two to their own devices, and I would suggest you do the same."

Lady Smithfield agreed quite readily, overcome with joy. It had been weighing on her mind all day that the match she had boasted of to Lady Abernathy and her niece was destined to come to nothing, and she would be humiliated in front of all her neighbors. It was quite a relief to think that she would not be made to eat humble pie.

The duke was pleased to see he had relieved his hostess's mind, but still could not be entirely easy until the entire truth was made known. But he comforted himself in that he had told the entire truth, though without specifying which daughter his son admired. With that consolation, and his hostess's expressions of delight following him up the stairs, he made his way to bed.

ഇരു

Emily found herself practicing the pianoforte more and more since her acquaintance with Alexander. She had even reflected on the fact that if she had conceived a hopeless passion for a gentleman at sixteen, she would be a regular virtuoso by now. She was engaged in this occupation when Alexander arrived at the Smithfield's on Saturday morning, anxious to put his fate to the touch.

When Wiggins would have announced him, Alexander begged him not to, and instead stood for almost a quarter of an hour, watching Emily play. If he hadn't been so in love, he would have been ashamed to observe her thus; for when playing her face was so expressive, her emotions so obvious, it was as if her soul was nakedly exposed. Totally unself-conscious, not aware she was being observed, her body was almost an extension of the music, and she swayed in a manner her mother would have been sure to denounce as vulgar had she been present.

When the piece she had been playing came to an end, Alexander spoke before she could begin another. "Emily."

Emily started, jumping up from the bench so quickly

she almost knocked it over. "Mr. Williams! You startled me."

"I apologize. Indeed, I did not know how to make you aware of my presence without startling you. You were so engrossed in the music."

Emily was embarrassed that he had observed her such, and hurried to invite him to sit down. "I am not sure where my mother and sister are this morning," she said. "I will have Wiggins call them." She moved as if to do so, and Alexander stopped her.

"Please do not. It is you I have come to see, and our privacy suits my purpose very well." Although he had just sat down, he jumped up and proceeded to pace back and forth, before startling her again by abruptly kneeling at her side.

"Emily. I have made no secret of my feelings for you. I admire you exceedingly, indeed, I love you. Would you do me the honor of becoming my wife?"

Emily did not know how to react. In all of her day-dreaming, she had never imagined quite this scene. She had been sure that Alexander had been trifling with her, and, because of this, had never envisioned he would propose to her. Now she was at a loss to know how to respond.

Alexander was not entirely daunted by her silence. He laughed a little nervously, and reminded her that it was generally considered good form to make a reply to an offer of marriage.

"I am sorry, it is just that I do not know how to respond," she answered in all honesty.

"Well, I am not an entirely disinterested party, but I think that an answer in the affirmative would be a good choice."

Emily looked into the handsome face, whose lines she had memorized, and wished with all her heart she could make such a reply. But her doubts were such that she knew they would have to be overcome before she could ever do so. "Believe me, I desire nothing more than to answer in the affirmative, but there are practical matters to consider."

Alexander rose, to sit in a nearby chair. "Practical matters?" he asked.

"Indeed. I am not sure if you know the extent of my dowry, but it is only two thousand pounds, and, as a curate, I cannot think you make more than fifty pounds a year. How are we to live on one hundred fifty pounds a year? *Where* are we to live? As romantic as it would seem to deny the importance of such matters in comparison with one's feelings, these things must be considered."

Alexander admitted to himself the truth of this statement, but wondered if this was a polite way of saying she would only marry a man of rank and fortune, no matter what her feelings. "I concede your point, but I would not propose if I did not have the means of taking care of you. Believe me when I say you will not want for anything."

This statement had the opposite effect for which it was intended. Emily, who was already suspicious of Alexander's source of income, felt he was as good as announcing that he was the highwayman. Her heart sank to hear him make such an announcement, but she was determined to uncover the truth.

"Might I inquire into the source of these means?"

Alexander looked uncomfortable, almost guilty,

which only confirmed Emily's suspicions. He could not think of a way of reassuring her without revealing the whole truth, and that would defeat the entire purpose of his charade. He wanted to hear she loved him as a curate, not as the heir to a dukedom. He began to grow angry that she was subjecting him to such an examination. When he had envisioned this scene, Emily had fallen gratefully into his arms, proclaiming her love and devotion for him. This inquisition was a far cry from what he had imagined.

"Why all these questions, Emily? Is your love granted only to a person who meets a certain annual income? What, have you decided you cannot admire someone with less than five thousand a year? Or perhaps you rate your charms even more highly than that. Perhaps you have determined that someone with less than ten thousand a year is completely beneath your notice. I should have realized such a thing when you plainly stated your intentions to steal your sister's intended husband."

Emily had never been so insulted in her life. "How dare you! For you to imply I am the type of woman to put a price tag on my favors. Why, you may as well call me a prostitute to my face! I will have you know, it is not your income that decided me against you, but your dishonesty and lack of candor. I cannot love a gentleman who would hide what he is."

Alexander looked shocked at this statement, wondering if she could be referring to his masquerade. No, he decided, it was merely an excuse on her part, to hide her mercenary motives. "So you cannot love me. One wonders, then, how well your plan to marry a certain marquess is unfolding. I assume, as his income is far in excess of ten thousand a year, you have irrevocably settled your heart on a brainless fop."

"You, sir, are as untrue to your so-called friends as you are to me. You do Lord Wesleigh an injustice when you describe him in such a manner."

"So I am correct. No lady could so nobly leap to a fellow's defense without already having decided to begin practicing for a lifetime of such a role. I wish you happy, my girl. I hope you will not live to regret your choice."

"If my choice is between you and him, than I cannot but make the wiser choice by choosing him."

"I think you have made your feelings, or lack thereof, abundantly clear. I will take my leave of you, and I can only regret that I ever entertained feelings for someone who would judge a man by his fortune."

He strode angrily from the room, leaving Emily alone. She began pacing the drawing room furiously, going over his insults in her head and telling herself she was glad she was to have nothing more to do with such a man. Her anger burned intensely for about a quarter of an hour after his departure, and she did not begin to regret her words until he had been gone for perhaps half an hour. It was only then that she remembered the light in his eyes as he had told her he loved her, and how that light had been extinguished completely by the end of their interview. Such thoughts could not but depress her, and she left the drawing room to go upstairs to her own chamber, where she proceeded to sob violently for what was left of the morning.

ളോൽ

Lady Smithfield found at dinner that evening that

both her daughters looked as sorrowful and lackluster as she had ever seen them. Both were pale and wan, with red, swollen eyes, and neither had more than a bite of dinner. She exchanged a look with the duke, but he persisted in being optimistic, and assured her when they were out of the girls' hearing that his daughter had looked just as pitiful scarcely a week before her engagement was announced.

"And she was normally as sensible a girl as you have ever seen. Don't know what it is exactly that makes them so silly when they fancy themselves in love, but I assure you, it's nothing out of the ordinary."

Lady Smithfield could not but reflect that she had not behaved in such a trying manner when Sir John had been courting *her*, but as her marriage was not what could be properly termed a love match, she felt herself unqualified to judge her daughters' behavior.

Sir Marcus had been sadly ignored by the entire Smithfield family that day, but as he had spent most of the previous night buying drinks for every riffraff and scamp in the county, he was not sorry to be left in solitude. He was hopeful of catching the highwayman that evening, so it would be his last day on a sickbed in any case.

Alexander sneaked into Marcus's chamber sometime after the household had gone to bed, determined to fulfill his promise to help Marcus catch the highwayman, but otherwise wanting very little to do with his erstwhile friend, who had stolen his ladylove in the most devious manner possible.

Marcus greeted Alexander with all the excitement of a gentleman who was about to perform an act of derring-do, but was quick to notice his friend did not share his high spirits. "You do not appear to be very excited for a man about to render a noble act for his country," he commented.

"Perhaps I do not share the same affinity for traitors as you do," Alexander replied, in his most cutting tone.

Marcus looked at Alexander in shock. "What the deuce is that supposed to mean?"

"I think you understand me."

"You think wrong. I have no idea what has got you in such high dudgeon. You haven't been drinking, have you? Because if you have, I'd rather you not join me this evening."

"I am not drunk. I am merely referring to your traitorous behavior in making up to the girl you knew I wished to marry."

"Not this again," Marcus replied, rolling his eyes in exasperation. "I told you, there was nothing to any of that. She was just playing some songs for me on the pianoforte. I will not ever listen to her play again, if you're going to make such a to-do about it. Why don't you just do as I suggested and make the girl an offer?"

"I did make her an offer. She said she was engaged to you."

Sir Marcus's thunderstruck expression proclaimed his innocence more than any words could have. "'Pon my word, the girl is a liar. I thought she was a decent girl, but it seems these girls today cannot tell the truth for anything. First Lady Cynthia, now Emily. Makes a man want nothing more to do with the gentler sex."

"Well, maybe she did not come right out and say you were engaged, but she implied it."

Marcus looked at Alexander skeptically. "Oho, implied it, did she? Same way she was throwing herself at me when she played the pianoforte for me, I suppose. Tell you what, Alexander, you've gone a bit daft over this girl. You're a regular demon of jealousy. A man can't even talk to the lady before you're imagining an intrigue."

"I did not imagine anything. She told me plainly were she to choose between the two of us, she would choose you."

Marcus tried to hide his pleasure in this comment, but failed miserably. "Did she, indeed? I never had a woman prefer me to you, at least not that I can remember, anyway. Daresay quite a few of them have, I just was not aware of it."

"As much as I hate to disappoint you, I am fairly sure it's not your golden curls that have inspired her to passion, but the fact that she thinks you a marquess, with a hefty allowance. In fact, I was almost positive that she returned my love, but apparently she is fonder of lucre than me."

"Well, I'm sorry you were crossed in love, old man, but perhaps apprehending a traitor to the crown will put you in a better mood."

Alexander agreed that nothing would bring him greater pleasure, and the gentlemen crept surreptitiously out of the chamber.

ℰℐℭℛ

Emily had not been able to sleep. Every time her eyes would close, *his* face would appear. She would hear him telling her again how much he admired and loved her.

And then she would see herself spouting some nonsense about *practical matters* when all she wanted to do was throw herself into his arms.

She reminded herself again that he was doomed to hang on the gibbet sooner or later, so it was probably better that she had ended it now, before matters had progressed even further. Then she would worry that perhaps he was not the highwayman after all, and she had allowed some silly suspicion to wreck all of her dreams.

She gave up any thought of sleep, and was just about to light a candle and attempt to read instead, when she heard a noise. Already out of bed, she hurried to the door and opened it a crack. She was not completely surprised to see Alexander shutting Lord Wesleigh's door, before the two crept through the hall and down the stairs.

As quickly as she could, she changed into an old gown and pelisse and quietly followed. She was sure they had exited by the kitchen door, at the back of the house, and she headed in that direction. Once outside the house, she heard them harnessing their horses, and waited until she saw them begin riding away, before she harnessed her own horse.

She took careful note of which direction they took, and was not surprised to see them take the Rye Road. That would be the obvious destination for a highwayman. But she had been extremely surprised to see Lord Wesleigh riding with Alexander. What was he doing assisting a highwayman in his criminal activity? Surely the heir to a dukedom would have no need to steal, and she thought Lord Wesleigh too scrupulous to do such a thing for a lark. Then again, young, idle gentlemen were

known to engage in many unscrupulous activities purely
to pass the time.

After waiting a few minutes to allow for some distance between them, Emily started out after the men. She
was thankful that the moon was almost full that night, so
she could clearly see the road. For some time she saw
nothing but the road curving ahead of her and the trees
crouching over her on each side. Finally, when she was
starting to wonder had she lost Alexander and Marcus
completely, she came to a straight stretch of road and
saw them plainly ahead of her. They had slowed down,
so she slowed down as well, careful to keep a bit of distance between them and her. If Alexander or Marcus saw
her, she would miss out on her chance to observe them
unnoticed. Her plan, hastily conceived, was to follow
them at a safe distance, and, when they reached the Rye
Road, wait unnoticed in the trees until something occurred.

There was also the possibility that she was mistaken,
and they were on their way to a tavern. However, they
were headed in the wrong direction if that was their plan.
They could not mean to ride all the way to Rye, at such
a late hour, when the tavern at Hawkhurst was so much
closer. No, she could only think of one reason they had
followed this route. Perhaps, when Alexander discovered
she knew what he was doing, she could persuade him to
give up such a life before anyone else caught him.

Her cogitation had kept her from dwelling on the
fact that she was riding alone, past midnight, in an area
frequented by highwaymen. Now, with her plan fixed
firmly in mind and nothing more to do than follow the
road, she began to think that perhaps she had not acted

very wisely.

She began to see things in the shadows and hear noises in the wood, and had to exercise the greatest self-control so as not to urge her horse on to greater speed and catch up with the gentlemen ahead of her, or, alternatively, to turn her horse around and head back home. Somehow, while in the midst of assuring herself she had gone too far to turn back, she stumbled on to the Rye Road before she expected to, with Alexander and Wesleigh nowhere in sight. She reined in, jumped down off her horse, and led her off into the woods by the road. She tried to proceed quietly, but a horse tromping through underbrush is bound to make noise, and she winced each time the mare took a step. She hoped against hope that Alexander and Wesleigh had not seen or heard her, and cursed her stupidity in not paying closer attention to her surroundings.

She had been waiting for a few minutes in the darkness, and had just convinced herself that no one had noticed her after all, when a man grabbed her around the chest and put his hand to her mouth.

Never in her life had Emily felt such fear. She had not heard or seen anyone coming, and in the shock of finding herself clasped against a man's chest, she instinctively yelled out, although with her mouth covered, it came out as no more than a whimper.

"Hush," said a harsh voice at her ear. She barely heard him, as by this time she began to fear she would suffocate, and had begun thrashing around, attempting to break his grip. "If I let you go, will you promise not to scream?" These words Emily did hear, and she nodded. The man released her mouth, but, with his hand now free, tied something about her wrists.

"What are you doing?" she asked him.

"I cannot risk you flying away on me, can I, my pretty ladybird?" he said, his breath hot on her neck.

Once she was capable of thinking, her first thought was that perhaps Alexander had crept up on her, and it was he who had her in his grip. However, that hope was now dispelled. Even though she could not see the man, she knew this was not Alexander or Marcus. However, they were in the woods somewhere nearby, and if she screamed loudly enough, perhaps they would come to her rescue. So, contrary to her promise, she opened her mouth and screamed as loud as she could.

"Why you little—" she heard her assailant say, before everything went black.

Eleven

৪৩

Alexander and Marcus heard Emily scream, but Marcus restrained Alexander from going to her rescue.

"Wait," Marcus said, grabbing Alexander by the arm as he pushed past him. "If we go thrashing through the woods, he'll be sure to hear us. If he does not know we are here, he will come out onto the road, and we can follow him."

"But that sounded like Emily."

"Perhaps it is Emily. She may have followed us from Smithfield House. However, we are liable to do more harm than good if we go off half-cocked."

Alexander, although he saw the wisdom of this, found it very frustrating to sit and do nothing while Emily was in the hands of some brute. Although it seemed a lifetime to Alexander, it was only a few moments later when a figure appeared on the road, leading a horse with a bulky object thrown over the saddle. As the highwayman could only proceed at a walk, Alexander and Marcus left their horses tethered to a tree and followed on foot.

The man led them on back roads to an abandoned building, which had been used at one time for textile manufacturing. He tied his horse in the back and, hefting Emily over his shoulder, entered the building.

Alexander and Marcus followed the highwayman
through the door and into the building. The interior was
in darkness, and they stopped just inside the door, listening for sounds of movement. After a few moments, they
heard some slight sounds, followed by the highwayman
asking was his little ladybird finally awake, before lighting a rushlight.

Alexander and Marcus walked stealthily toward the
light, but, not as familiar with the place as the highwayman, Alexander bumped into an old loom, which fell
over with a clatter and alerted the highwayman to their
approach.

The highwayman quickly extinguished the light, but
Alexander and Marcus rushed in that direction, oblivious
to any bumps and bruises they sustained in the process.
They felt around in the darkness, finally finding the flint
and tinder, but, after striking it, they were amazed to
find the highwayman and Emily were nowhere to be
found.

"What happened to them?" Alexander asked in be-
wilderment.

Marcus said nothing, looking around them. "It looks
like he's been sleeping here," he told Alexander, pointing
to a makeshift cot. "However, it looks like nothing more
than a pied-à-terre. He's definitely hiding the booty
somewhere else." He raised the rushlight, but they saw
nothing more than a pile of blankets and some empty
bottles.

Alexander, who could not understand how a man
and woman could so completely disappear, ran back outside the building to verify that the highwayman's horse
was still tied. Finding the horse docilely eating some

grass, he went back inside just in time to see Marcus lifting something off the floor. As Alexander got closer, he realized it was a door. When he finally joined Marcus, he saw he had uncovered some kind of underground tunnel.

"What the deuce!" Alexander exclaimed, and prepared to lower himself into the tunnel.

Once again, Marcus restrained him. "Wait. This is one of the tunnels that lead to the Tudor Arms in Hawkhurst. I think, rather than following him when he is most likely quite far ahead by now, we should go directly to the Tudor Arms and await him on the other end."

"What if you are mistaken and it leads somewhere else? Meanwhile, he has Emily down there with him. Tell you what, you go to the Tudor Arms, I'll go through the tunnel. That way one of us is bound to catch him." Alexander was gone into the tunnel before Marcus had time to agree or disagree. Marcus, having left his horse tethered to a tree, took the highwayman's horse, and rode as fast as he could to the Tudor Arms.

Alexander found himself in a narrow passage, cold and dank, through which he had to travel bent forward, as it was too low to walk upright. He had extinguished his light, so he was in complete darkness, and he walked with his hands outstretched, guiding him. All he could think with each labored step was how terrified Emily must be, and, although his inclination was to run as fast as he could, he forced himself to walk slowly and carefully. It would not do Emily any good were he to hit his head in the darkness and be rendered unconscious.

After a stretch of time that seemed interminable to

him, but was probably only about fifteen minutes, he heard some noises and knew they were just ahead. Emily had impeded the man's progress quite a bit, and Alexander could hear him warning her to hurry.

"I should've left you back there, and if I wasn't such a fool for the ladies, I would've. But you seemed such a nice cozy armful, it seemed a shame to leave you behind for those clumsy oafs."

Emily, gagged as she was, said nothing in reply. She felt as though she had stumbled into a horrible nightmare and could not believe it was all really happening. The blow to her head had left her a little dazed, as well, which also contributed to her sense of unreality. She stumbled along the narrow tunnel as best she could, which was made even more difficult by the fact that her hands were tied behind her back. Again and again she cursed her stupidity in venturing alone into an area known to be frequented by a highwayman. Her wretched suspicions of Alexander had led her into such a dangerous situation, and she wondered how she could have ever believed him guilty of such a thing. She wished she could go back in time to that morning, where she would give a very different answer to his question, thereby avoiding the situation she now found herself in.

She refused to think of what this man had in store for her and concentrated on the hope that Alexander and Marcus would somehow catch up with them. She prayed that they had been the ones who had chased them into this tunnel.

She did not know whether to be relieved or terrified when they finally reached their destination. She had begun to feel she would go insane if they had stayed in the dark and musty tunnel a moment longer. Being gagged with one's hands tied was unpleasant enough, but being in a narrow, short space on top of it contributed to her feeling of suffocation, until she felt that something inside her was about to explode. Before this could happen, however, the highwayman had untied her hands and was pushing her up, out of the tunnel.

"Pull yourself up by your hands," he told her. She obeyed eagerly, but until the highwayman also came out of the tunnel and lit a lamp, she had no idea if her present situation was any better than the one she had just left. When the lamp was lit, she saw she was in a small chamber of some kind. She looked around for a door, but the room did not appear to possess doors or windows. There was a bed, a table with one chair, and a chest. She looked with interest at the highwayman, as well, who had joined her in the small room. This was the first time she had seen his face since he had abducted her. He looked to be about thirty-five, with dark hair and eyes. He was not horribly disfigured in any way, and was probably considered by many to be handsome. Emily, however, viewed his appearance with dislike, thinking how wrong the reports were that labeled him a gentleman. The highwayman told her to sit down, and she sat down at the table, wondering if she dare undo her gag now that her hands were free. Before she had time to act on the thought, the highwayman removed it for her.

"You can scream all you want now, my girl. There's not anyone who will hear you, and if they did, they would not be able to find you."

"Where are we?" she asked, although she scarcely recognized her voice for her own.

"Welcome to the Tudor Arms," he said, with a flourish. He laughed as she looked around her in confusion. "We're in a small room that adjoins the basement. It was used by the Hawkhurst Gang sixty or seventy years ago. It is generally known that the tunnels exist, and even that they used to lead to the Tudor Arms, but no one other than I has seen the inside of this room for sixty years. There's another tunnel that leads out of here, much shorter than the one we took in." He gestured to the wall opposite, and Emily saw what looked like a hole in the wall. "It leads to the stables. Very convenient for me, as I leave my horse stabled there." To Emily's dismay, he stopped talking and approached the table where she sat, holding the lamp up to her face. "Let's see how I made out this evening." Emily set in silence, petrified, as he studied her face. "I'd say I have got quite a jewel here, and I didn't even have to rob a carriage." He laughed at his little joke, and Emily found the courage to speak.

"Sir, I am related to the nobility. It will fare badly for you if you kidnap me. We have a duke in residence at our home as I speak. And his son, a marquess, is my betrothed. They would be quite concerned if anything happened to me," Emily warned, heedless of the truth. She would have said she was married to the Prince Regent if she thought that would have deterred him.

The highwayman just laughed at her threats. "You think to scare me with a duke and marquess, do you? I lost my fear of the nobility long ago. My father was agent at a grand estate, and I have a fine lord in my pocket."

"What do you mean?" Emily asked, although she was really not interested. However, she figured if she kept him talking, he would not touch her.

Alexander, on the other hand, was very interested. He was still in the tunnel, waiting for a good opportunity to come out. He crouched just below the exit, where the light could not touch him, and listened carefully.

"I mean that a certain lord supplies me with details of when particular information is to be carried, by whom it is to be carried, and what route they are to take. I obtain this information for him, and, in return, he rewards me handsomely."

"To whom do you refer?" Emily asked, a little curious by this point, but mostly to keep him talking. The highwayman looked at Emily for a moment, as if trying to decide whether to share such a secret, and then shrugged. "I suppose it will do no harm to tell you, and as fond of titles as you are, you may be acquainted. Lord Cecil Burke, youngest son of the earl of Kilburne."

Emily thought for a moment, as she did not recognize the name at first. "Of course, Lord Cecil," she said, as she recollected him. "He's a cousin or nephew, a connection at least, of Lord Abernathy. But I do not understand. What information is it that he desires to obtain?"

The highwayman smiled. "I am glad you are stupid, my little ladybird. I detest any sign of intelligence in females. Let me break it down for you. We are presently at war, and one side will always pay a great deal to know what the other side is doing. Lord Cecil, for want of ready cash, makes the information available to the other side."

"With your assistance. You are despicable. A filthy traitor."

"Yes, well, unfortunately many in England share

your sentiments, which is why I have decided on a change of climate. I have enough money to live quite comfortably in France the rest of my days, and, while you may view me as a traitor, they must, of course, view me differently. I had decided to leave tonight, but I really did not fancy speaking French the rest of my life. Your arrival upon the scene was quite fortuitous; I will have a little bit of England to take with me, as well as someone to warm my bed at night."

It was all Alexander could do to restrain himself from leaping out of his hiding place, particularly when he heard sounds of a struggle. Just as he was preparing to exit, he heard a slap and Emily's voice. "You swine," she said.

"Call me Jack," he said, rubbing his cheek where she had slapped him. "If I wasn't fond of a bit of a tussle, you'd have your hands tied up again, my girl. Now then, before we get to know each other better, I have a little chore for you." Jack went over to the chest and opened it, removing a piece of paper and a pen. "You are to write your parents, or whoever you think may be concerned about you, and tell them that you have run away with your secret lover, the son of an estate agent. If I know the nobility, they will write you off with barely a sigh of regret."

"You cannot make me write such a thing," Emily protested.

"Oh, can't I? How would you fancy a bruise on your other cheek, to match this one?" he asked, touching the spot where he'd hit her earlier. "You will write whatever I say, or pay the consequences."

Emily took the paper and pen and began writing.

Alexander removed his pistol from his coat pocket, as he had heard all he needed to, and it did not appear Marcus was going to come to his assistance. He heard the highwayman tell Emily that she needn't write a book, that he had other plans for the night, and Alexander cocked his pistol. When he heard sounds of a scuffle, and Emily's cries of distress, he scrambled out of the tunnel as quickly as possible.

The highwayman did not even notice him, so intent was he on Emily. He had his arms around her and was pressing his lips to her neck, and the expression of revulsion and fear on Emily's face was something Alexander felt would live in his memory long after that night was over. He stepped up behind the man and shoved the pistol into his back. "Let go of her, and put your hands up where I can see them."

The highwayman obeyed, and just as Alexander was checking his pockets for weapons, they were all distracted by a very loud banging noise, before the wall of the room came crashing in on them.

Twelve

୧ର

Marcus had rushed to the Tudor Arms, where he had asked to speak to the landlord of the establishment. The landlord was helpful enough, and agreed that it was common knowledge that the Hawkhurst Gang had used a tunnel that was supposed to end at his establishment, but he had never seen any evidence of such a tunnel.

"Believe me, your honor, if there was such a thing, I would know it. Know every square inch of this place, I do."

Marcus thanked him, but asked him if he could perform his own investigation, just the same. The landlord agreed, and Marcus asked to be directed to the basement. He reasoned that as the tunnel ran underground, it was likely to end below ground, as well. He took a lamp and examined each wall in the basement. His first time around he could find nothing, and was worried he was wasting precious time on a wild-goose chase. He asked the landlord, who had been observing him in silence, if the basement ran the entire length of the building.

The landlord answered in the affirmative, and watched in puzzlement as Marcus began to measure off the distance of one side of the room by placing one foot in front of the other and counting. He then asked for the quickest way out of the building and began measuring the outside wall in the same manner. When he was finished, he looked at the landlord in triumph.

"Even allowing for the width of the outside walls, there's still a good ten-foot difference between the length of your basement and the length of the building."

The landlord proclaimed his astonishment and directed some of the servants to assist Marcus in investigating the walls of the basement. It was not long before someone noticed an irregularity in one wall, and Marcus drew closer to investigate. It looked as if someone had applied stucco over the stone wall in this one section. Marcus asked for a knife, and began to chip away at the stucco. After a few minutes, he had chipped away about a square inch or so, and saw that there was wood beneath. "I believe, gentleman," he told his audience, who were waiting to hear the results of his investigation, "we have found a door."

Marcus asked if they had anything they could use as a battering ram. There was a long log in the woodshed that had not yet been cut up for firewood that was found to suit this purpose. Marcus organized the two servants who looked the strongest to begin battering down the door. After just two tries they were successful, and the door gave way, the log flying through with the two men dragged along behind.

Inside the room, all was in chaos. Alexander had dropped the highwayman and his pistol, grabbing Emily and pulling her out of the way of the log. The highwayman, seeing his chance for escape, ran into the tunnel that led to the stable. But Marcus, who had entered the room by this time, managed to grab him by the back of his coat and hold him for the few seconds necessary until the other men came through the broken wall and assisted him in dragging the highwayman back into the room. Then they tied his hands behind him, with the same length of rope that had just recently been around Emily's wrists. The men who had formed part of the battering ram were dazed, bruised, and a little scratched, but otherwise all right, and Marcus promised them a guinea and a pint for their assistance in catching a traitor to the crown.

Emily was crying in Alexander's arms, hardly able to believe her ordeal was over. Alexander held her tightly against his chest, telling her to hush, and gently smoothing her hair back from her face. He kept seeing in his mind her expression as the highwayman held her captive in his arms, and he tightened his hold until Emily was in more danger from suffocation from him than she had been in the tunnel.

The landlord approached them, to offer Emily a room for the night and ask if he should send for the doctor.

"No. No, thank you. I want to go home," Emily said, disengaging herself from Alexander's embrace and attempting to compose herself.

"Emily, it is nearly three in the morning, and you have sustained a blow to the head. I really think you should stay here," Alexander told her.

"I just want to go home," she replied, looking up at him through eyes that shone with tears, about to lose her thin grip on her composure. Alexander sighed, and told the landlord he would see the lady home, but asked him if he could make arrangements for a chaise.

As Alexander and Emily were leaving, Marcus

stopped them to ask Emily if she was all right. She thanked him for his concern, but told him that Alexander had arrived just in time, leaving Marcus to wonder that she gave all the credit to Alexander when it was he who had knocked down a wall to come to her rescue.

Alexander took a moment to tell Sir Marcus what he had overheard the highwayman tell Emily about Lord Cecil Burke. Marcus thanked him, happy to have the information he needed without having to interrogate the man himself.

The ride back to Smithfield House was accomplished in near silence. Emily was thinking that, since she now knew Alexander was not the highwayman, a renewal of his addresses would not be looked down upon. Alexander was remembering that she had told the highwayman she was engaged to a marquess, and wondered then why she had thrown herself into his arms instead of Marcus's. Of course, he may have been the one to initiate the embrace; everything had happened so fast he could not recall exactly.

As he was not aware that Emily had suspected him of being a criminal, nothing had changed in his mind. Emily had refused him. As hard as it was for him to believe, she did not really love him. Now that the highwayman had been captured, there was no reason for him to persist in his charade. The truth could be told, and he could leave Stonehurst and return to London. That thought brought him little pleasure. The only thought that pleased him in the least was the fact that Emily was bound to bitterly regret her choice when she discovered who he actually was.

It was after three in the morning when Emily finally returned home, to everyone's shock and dismay. Her mother was more shocked than anyone, as her daughter had returned in company with a lone gentleman, which meant her reputation was in shreds.

Emily, who wanted nothing more than to go upstairs, wash her mouth out with strong soap, and sink into an exhausted slumber, was forced to meet her mother and sister in the drawing room and try to answer their multitude of questions. She was very thankful when Alexander put an end to the barrage by telling them simply, "She was abducted by a highwayman, but, Sir Ma——, that is, Lord Wesleigh and I were able to recover her before any damage was done. Now, I am sure she would like nothing more than to have a good rest, after which she will be able to give more intelligent replies to your request for information. I will return tomorrow afternoon to provide any more explanations you may require."

Lady Smithfield, though bursting with questions, had to be satisfied for the nonce, and Emily whispered her gratitude to Alexander before turning to leave. She was struck by a sudden thought, and turned back to Alexander, "My horse," she said, so tired it came out as barely a whisper.

"Not to worry. I am on my way to collect the horses now."

Emily nodded, too tired to thank him, and turned to walk up the stairs to her bedchamber.

଼ଉଅ

It was almost noon before she awoke the next day,

and at first she could not imagine why her jaw ached so. Then the activities of the previous evening returned to her with a rush, and she closed her eyes again, trying to take them all in. She had been abducted by a highwayman, but Alexander had saved her, and as he was not the highwayman himself, she was actually in a better humor than she had been in four-and-twenty hours earlier.

She quickly washed and dressed, and, as she was finishing, Lydia entered her chamber.

"Emily! You are awake! I am so glad. Mama just sent me to awaken you. How are you feeling?"

"My jaw aches a little, but other than that I am remarkably well."

Lydia took a closer look at Emily's face. She and her mother had not seen Emily's injury when she was brought home, and she was shocked by the black-and-blue mark on Emily's cheek. "Oh, Emily! You poor thing, it must have been perfectly dreadful," Lydia exclaimed sympathetically.

"It was, and I am very relieved the whole thing is over. If Mr. Williams had not come, I would be unfortunate indeed," Emily said with a shudder.

"But, Emily, none of us can work out how it is the highwayman abducted you. Surely he did not come to the house."

"No, he did not. I behaved very stupidly, I am sorry to say."

"Emily, you did not agree to meet him clandestinely!"

"No, no, of course not. I am not *that* stupid. However, I rode out to the Rye Road and hid in the bushes, in the hopes of observing who the highwayman was. I thought perhaps it was someone I was acquainted with, in which case I could inform the authorities. Unfortunately, the highwayman discovered my hiding place and rendered me unconscious. Mr. Williams and Lord Wesleigh heard me scream and followed us until they had an opportunity to rescue me."

"But I still do not understand. How could Mr. Williams and Lord Wesleigh have heard you scream? You do not mean that they were at the Rye Road as well?"

"Yes, that is how I arrived there. I followed them."

"You followed them? But why? I thought you went to observe the highwayman," Lydia asked, more confused than ever.

"I did, but it all started when I saw Williams and Wesleigh leave the house, and that is what gave me the idea of going also." Emily knew her jumbled explanation was hardly convincing, but she did not want to admit that she had followed the men because she had believed Williams was the highwayman. Lydia was forced to be content with this explanation, such as it was, and Emily left her to go downstairs and have a late breakfast.

While she was eating, her jaw aching with every bite, her mother came into the room to tell her to hurry, that the duke, Lord Wesleigh, Mr. Williams, and Mr. Sedgewick all awaited her in the drawing room. Emily was not anxious to meet that particular group of gentleman, nor was she at all eager to answer the many questions that were sure to be asked, but she could not see that she had any other choice than to obey her mother's dictum.

Her eyes flew to Alexander's as soon as she entered the room, but it was the duke who, upon seeing her, immediately came to greet her.

"My dear girl," he told her, taking her hand and patting it as he spoke to her. "I am so pleased that you suffered no ill consequences from your misadventure."

Emily thanked him for his kindness, and went to sit beside Lydia. She was very embarrassed by his sympathy, as she had begun to think of her actions as those of an undisciplined hoyden. She hated to think what her mother would have to say on the subject, and made herself as inconspicuous as possible on the sofa, hoping no one would ask her why she had behaved in so reckless a manner.

Lady Smithfield begged the gentlemen to be seated, and when they were, the duke said he had an announcement to make. Lydia, whose own troubles loomed larger in her mind than anything else, was sure it was to be an announcement of her betrothal to the marquess. Before the duke could make his announcement, she stated in a clear voice that only trembled slightly that she was prepared to do her duty.

While the rest of the party looked at her in surprise, the duke and his son wondering what in the world the girl was blathering on about, Sir Marcus rightly guessed her meaning. "You look like Joan of Arc about to be burned alive at the stake. Such martyrdom is not necessary, my girl. I would as lief marry my housekeeper as you."

Lady Smithfield looked quite offended at this plain speaking, and seemed as if she might object, turning to the duke for support. Before she could say anything, however, Sedgewick confronted Sir Marcus, righteous indignation clearly written on his face.

"You, sir, are a fool, to esteem so high an honor so lightly. Why, if I were in your position, I would thank God every day for giving me the opportunity to just be in Miss Smithfield's presence, regardless of whether or not she ever learned to return my affections."

"What noble sentiments! Sir, you put me to the blush," Lydia stated, a slight smile appearing as she addressed him.

"Miss Smithfield, the sentiments I expressed are totally sincere. If only I could say to you all that is in my heart."

"I wish you could as well." Lydia and Sedgewick stared at each other mournfully, their audience forgotten.

"Why can he not?" Emily interceded, startling the two young lovers, who jumped in surprise.

"What?" Sedgewick asked.

"Why can't you tell Lydia what is in your heart? What is preventing you?"

Sedgewick was very obviously put out by Emily's interference in an important scene between him and Lydia. "It is quite obvious what prevents me. She is betrothed to another."

"That is correct," Lady Smithfield interjected. She had been watching the spectacle before her with dismay, unable to believe all her hopes and dreams were being dashed to pieces. Her eldest daughter, who had always done what was expected of her, was apparently contemplating throwing herself away on a vicar when she might marry the heir to a dukedom. "Lydia is betrothed to this gentleman, and the announcement is to be made later this month." She gestured toward Marcus, before looking to the duke for confirmation of her statement.

The duke cleared his throat and looked uncomfortable. "Yes, well, perhaps the announcement I was about to make will help clear matters up a little." There was a long pause as the duke collected his thoughts, and all in the room turned to look at him expectantly. "As you all know, the highwayman that had been causing such terror in the neighborhood was apprehended last night. What most of you do not know is that he was also involved in espionage, spying for the French. My son and his friend, Sir Marcus Reddings, were forced to assume another identity in order to help apprehend the traitor. Unfortunately, this meant that we had to deceive you all, as well. For that I am truly sorry. The gentleman who you have assumed to be my son, Lord Wesleigh, is in actuality, Sir Marcus Reddings. And the gentleman that has introduced himself to you as Mr. Alexander Williams, is my son, Lord Wesleigh."

There was a shocked silence as all in the room attempted to digest these words. When they had, their reactions were so diverse and unexpected as to be comical.

Lady Smithfield was quite disappointed in losing Sir Marcus as a son-in-law. When he stood next to his friend, arrayed in such vibrant colors, with his golden curls tousled and the jewel in his cravat catching the sunlight, she felt that the true Lord Wesleigh paled into insignificance beside him. However, as it was obvious Lydia did *not* care for Sir Marcus, maybe the match had a chance of proceeding with a different groom.

Lydia was completely thrown by the announcement. As Sir Marcus had appeared in all her musings as the monster intent on tearing her from the arms of her true love, it was disconcerting, to say the least, to discover he had never had such an intention. And as she had noticed Lord Wesleigh, in his role as curate, had paid far greater attention to Emily than herself, she was totally at a loss to know how to proceed. She felt as an actress would were she to walk out on stage to discover the cast was performing in a play to which she had not learned the lines.

Emily, whom Alexander was observing intently to gauge her reaction, was simply horrified. Her first thought was that she had boasted to this man that she intended to marry him for his title and his fortune. She was thoroughly embarrassed, and wanted nothing more than to run from the room and pursue her thoughts in solitude. Her next thought was that he had asked her to marry him, and she had refused, and he would never believe now that she did so because she thought him to be a highwayman. He would, of course, think it was because she was more concerned about rank and fortune than mutual love and esteem. Oh, why had she not told him her suspicions last night in the carriage! Now it was too late, as he would never renew his addresses to a female he suspected would marry him merely for the sake of his money. She had to use all the self-control in her possession to school her features into an appearance of calmness, as she was conscious that she must maintain her composure so that no one in the room would suspect anything was amiss.

Alexander was unable to tell what Emily was thinking. Her face, expressive as ever, had registered shock, maybe even embarrassment, but she had only looked once in his direction, and in that moment, it seemed to him her eyes were filled with pain. She had looked away almost at once, and now would not glance his way, gazing intently down at her hands instead, which were folded in her lap.

After allowing the shock of his first bit of news to subside, the duke continued. "Another happy result of the masquerade was the discovery that Miss Smithfield appears to have formed a prior attachment which, of course, would nullify any match between her and my son. I am sure that her mother and I never had any intention of causing unhappiness when we fostered the idea of an engagement between Miss Smithfield and Lord Wesleigh. On the contrary, we only want the happiness and contentment of our children, and of course that could only be found by marrying where your heart leads you."

Lady Smithfield heard the second announcement with far more shock than she had the first. She would be a laughingstock. All of her dreams, her plans for her daughter, had come to nothing. Her beautiful daughter, the pride of her mother, was to marry a vicar. How Lady Abernathy would crow. But then Lady Smithfield happened to look at her daughter. Lydia had at first been sitting in stunned disbelief, but soon afterward an expression of such sweet happiness transformed her face she was more beautiful than she had ever been. Certainly, when Lady Smithfield compared her current expression with what it had been the past week or so, it was obvious that she had not been looking out for her daughter's best interests. And Sedgewick was a handsome fellow, she thought, looking him over critically. She really did prefer fair-haired gentlemen. Perhaps Sir Marcus might be persuaded to give Sedgewick the name of his tailor . . .

After a few minutes, Lady Smithfield was so reconciled to the match that she persuaded Lydia and Sedgewick to retire to the morning room, where they might enjoy some privacy from the rest of the group. She also began to think of asking the duke when the living at Silverden, his country estate, would be available, for that was a far more prestigious living than the one there in Stonehurst, and he might be persuaded to give it to Sedgewick. When she finally did get the opportunity to ask him, she was quite disappointed to hear that the current occupant was in robust health, and only forty years of age at the very most.

When Lydia and Sedgewick left the room, Emily felt she, too, could leave without occasioning any comment, and she soon took her leave of the gentlemen, murmuring something about some chore she had to perform.

It was obvious to Alexander that Emily was laboring under some strong emotion, but, as he was convinced it was no more than her regret in losing out on his fortune, he was not too sympathetic. He would allow her to suffer a little, as he had suffered by her refusal, but, in the back of his mind, he felt he would marry her in the end. He soon took his leave, and, when Lady Smithfield issued him an invitation to stay, he thanked her but told her he was quite comfortable with Sedgewick. Lady Smithfield was somewhat relieved by his refusal, as her small house was almost filled to capacity with her current guests and their retinue of servants. Sir Marcus, on the other hand, was happy to agree to an extended stay, at least until after the Abernathys' ball, which he had every expectation of being invited to once he paid a call at Rothergate. He soon took his leave as well, mentioning that he had to travel to London immediately, but he would be returning the next day. His departure left the duke and Lady Smithfield by themselves.

"Well. It was quite a morning for surprises," said Lady Smithfield.

"Yes, indeed," the duke agreed. "I hope you were not discomposed by the announcements."

"Well, I must admit, I was a little peeved just at first. I daresay it slipped your mind, but you assured me only yesterday that your son was in love with my daughter."

"And so he is," the duke said affably.

Lady Smithfield looked at him in wonder, thinking perhaps he was as mad as old King George. "You just made an announcement to the opposite."

"Lady Smithfield," the duke said, quite gently, "you do, I believe, have *two* daughters?"

It took Lady Smithfield a moment to grasp the significance of this statement, and, when she had, she was beside herself. "My dear duke, you mean he loves Emily? Why, I never once suspected. But, then, she was not herself yesterday, and I did wonder when you said that about young girls in love, with whom *Emily* could be in love. Oh, my, I cannot take it in. Both my daughters married! And I will no longer have to fear what Lady Abernathy has to say. As if your son could be the least interested in that cold niece of hers! I knew it was a falsehood from the very start." Lady Smithfield's exclamations and rhapsodizing went on for a good five minutes, until the duke interrupted her to tell her there was nothing settled as of yet, and she was not to mention it to Emily, or anyone else.

"Not mention it? What do you mean?"

"Well, my son had this notion of testing her love for him, and so proposed to her while he was still in the guise of a curate. Emily refused, for whatever reason, but now he's convinced she acted from mercenary motives. I think it will take him a little while to cool off and approach her again."

Lady Smithfield could not quite comprehend what the duke was saying. Of course Emily had refused a curate. She was surprised her daughter had acted with such good sense. It was unfortunate, of course, that the young man had later turned out to be a marquess, but Emily could not have known such a thing at the time. Why Lord Wesleigh would hold such a thing against her daughter was something she could not understand. However, the duke reminded her that she had promised to let the young couple pursue their courtship without interference, so she agreed to be patient for a little while longer.

Thirteen
ဢၣၩ

Lydia sought Emily out after Sedgewick had left, eager to tell her all the details of his proposal and her acceptance. Emily, despite her own unhappiness, managed to show her genuine joy at her sister's engagement, and listened unselfishly to every minute detail. She was sure Sedgewick was happy as well, but suspected he would have been happier if he had had to overcome further obstacles in his pursuit of Lydia. Emily was beginning to think he enjoyed being the object of a tragic love affair far more than a happy one.

Lydia was so preoccupied with her own happiness that it was some time before she realized that there was something troubling her sister. Gradually, however, as the first rush of confidences subsided, she began to notice that her sister was quieter than usual, and that her smiles, while sincere, had a wistful quality about them. Emily was relieved to be asked what was troubling her, and described the whole sorry business from start to finish.

"So, that is that," she finished, with resignation. "He will have nothing more to do with me, and how can I blame him? He thinks me another Lady Cynthia."

"But, Emily, I am sure if you just explained *why* you refused him—"

"How would he ever believe me? No, the time to tell him was the night of my rescue. I hesitated, and now I am lost."

"I cannot believe that he has ceased to love you. I am sure he would be relieved to hear your explanation."

"Perhaps. I feel, however, that I have lost him irrevocably. There is no warmth in his regard any longer, not like there was. And then, after my foolish behavior in traveling unaccompanied after dark, he probably thinks my actions completely inexplicable. Certainly they were lacking in the decorum one looks for in the wife of a marquess, not to mention a future duchess. No, I must forget him," Emily announced resolutely, and when Lydia looked disbelieving, Emily just smiled. "You do not believe me, I see. Well, I am determined. I am only nineteen after all, and Lord Wesleigh is not the only gentleman in the world. I am going to a ball on Wednesday, where I am sure to meet a number of nice gentlemen. I refuse to let Lord Wesleigh destroy my pleasure in the ball. I just hope my bruise has faded by then." This effectively turned the subject to that of cosmetics that could be discreetly applied to disguise Emily's bruise, if necessary, followed by a serious discussion of how each of them should arrange her hair.

Lydia, however, could not be happy when her sister suffered so miserably. She resolved to do something about it, and consulted Sedgewick at the earliest opportunity. He was happy at the prospect of interfering in his friend's romance as thoroughly as Wesleigh had interfered with his own, and he and Lydia soon decided the most effective way of inciting Wesleigh to passion was to make him jealous.

"But of whom?" Lydia asked, once this course was decided upon.

"There are sure to be quite a few gentlemen at the ball."

"Yes, but I know of no one in particular who admires Emily."

"Wesleigh does not know that. We just have to pick out one of her partners, and I will mention to Wesleigh that he has told me how greatly he admires Emily."

"Jonathan," Lydia exclaimed, admiration shining in her eyes, "you are brilliant."

This statement was bound to make Sedgewick forget his friend's ill-fated romance completely, and the conversation was effectively over.

⁎⁎⁎

It was not to be imagined, however, that the two unfortunate lovers were not thrown together often before the ball on Wednesday evening. The duke was still Lady Smithfield's guest, Alexander was now acknowledged as his son, and Sedgewick was engaged to one of the daughters of the house. This made for many unpleasant meetings between Emily and Alexander. Added to this were the obvious matchmaking efforts of Lydia and Sedgewick, and the less obvious efforts of Lady Smithfield and the duke. Sir Marcus was the only person who had no interest in seeing Emily and Wesleigh get together.

For Sir Marcus fancied himself quite smitten with Emily Smithfield in his own right. He had been previously well disposed toward her for her concern for him when he had been restricted to his bedchamber, but upon learning that she favored him, as Wesleigh had assured him she did, he began to see her as a female of great discernment. There was also some romance in his arriving in the nick of time to wrest her from the arms of her captor (as he persisted in thinking he was her true rescuer, whatever Wesleigh might think). However, it was her behavior since that time that he found truly entrancing. He sensed a softer quality in her since the abduction and, not realizing she was in the throes of despair, felt that perhaps her adventure had changed her in some way. For, although he had liked Emily previously, he had not been as charmed by her vivaciousness of manner as Wesleigh had. He still recalled her theft of his quizzing glass with a shudder.

Tuesday, the day before the ball, it was decided the group would take an excursion to Bodiam Castle. Lady Smithfield was hopeful that the romantic setting would inspire Lord Wesleigh to propose to Emily. Lydia and Sedgewick hoped similarly, and resolved to somehow leave the two of them alone together. Sir Marcus likewise saw it as the perfect place for a proposal, and had determined to use the opportunity to make Emily an offer of marriage.

The day was fine, and the scenery exquisite, and even Emily felt her spirits begin to revive. She and Alexander were still only engaged in exchanging comments about the weather, but the atmosphere was charged with emotion, and Emily felt that anything could happen.

Everyone partook of a picnic luncheon, and Emily felt Alexander's eyes on her quite a few times throughout the meal. She and Alexander said very little, but Emily found herself laughing a few times at some of the duke's remarks, and it felt good to laugh again.

After lunch, Lydia and Sedgewick decided to take a walk about the grounds, and invited the others to join them. Lady Smithfield and the duke immediately declined, preferring to rest after their meal. Emily agreed, a little hesitantly, looking at Alexander in an attempt to gauge his reaction. He agreed readily, and Lydia and Sedgewick felt their scheme to be proceeding well, when, to everyone's dismay, Sir Marcus announced his intention of joining them. There was little to be done but acquiesce with good grace, and they all began their walk, Lydia and Sedgewick first, with Alexander, Emily, and Sir Marcus trailing behind.

After they had gone a short distance, Lydia mentioned she had left her sketchbook in the carriage, and she would like to make a drawing. She asked Sedgewick to accompany her to retrieve it, but insisted the others continue with their walk. While she was unable to leave Emily and Alexander completely alone, she trusted that Sir Marcus would realize what they were hoping to accomplish and withdraw on his own.

Sir Marcus, however, saw their removal as instrumental in assisting him in carrying out his plan, and was determined to rid himself of his friend's unwelcome presence. Pointing something out to Emily in the distance, so that she walked a little away from him and Alexander, he lowered his voice and told Alexander to make himself scarce.

"I beg your pardon?" Alexander asked.

"I am going to put my luck to the touch. I don't want you around spoiling the moment."

"Of course," Alexander said. "Forgive me for being so obtuse." Emily had begun walking back toward the gentlemen, having looked in vain for the black swan Sir Marcus had thought he had seen in the moat. Alexander bowed to her, telling her he must see to his father, and left her and Sir Marcus alone.

Emily was quite disappointed, but did not want to spoil Sir Marcus's pleasure. So she asked him would he like to turn back like the rest, or continue their walk. She was quite shocked when he led her over to a patch of grass and laid down a handkerchief, where he carefully placed one knee.

"Miss Smithfield, Emily, I feel that my admiration for you cannot have gone unobserved, you must realize how ardently I admire you."

When Emily shook her head no, and would have stopped him from speaking further, he interrupted her. "Your modesty does you credit. You could not but be aware that I have loved you from the first moment I laid eyes upon you. Well, perhaps not the first moment, because, as I recall, you were laughing at me for observing you through my quizzing glass while wearing green glasses, but shortly after that," he asserted, before realizing that he had not actually loved her until very recently. He then became tangled up in an explanation of how, even though her gall in stealing his quizzing glass had offended him, he was willing to overlook her natural high spirits, and that he was sure she would appear much more fashionable once she had a London modiste. Just as he realized that he had not yet asked her the all-important question, he was interrupted by a stifled giggle.

He stopped in mid-sentence, looking at Emily in disbelief. Surely she had not *giggled* in the middle of his marriage proposal? But when he reached for his quizzing glass to observe Emily's expression more closely, she could no longer restrain herself and was soon laughing uncontrollably.

"Well!" he said, highly offended, and stood up, picking up the handkerchief he had been kneeling on, and waving it in the air to remove any dirt or straw, before folding it and returning it to his pocket. "I am glad you stopped me before I actually offered for you! I could never be married to someone who is so lacking in delicacy that she actually *giggled* in the middle of a marriage proposal! Every feeling must be offended."

Emily attempted to apologize, but when Sir Marcus began to mutter how he should have known better than to ever think they would have suited, and she hadn't even let him win at chess, she gave up the attempt as useless. However, she did do her best to maintain her composure, with only a slight shaking of her shoulders to betray her, until they returned to the rest of the party.

Alexander was not with the others, as he could not bear to be present when Sir Marcus and Emily returned, and their engagement was announced. He hoped Emily would refuse Marcus, but when he remembered how she had stated quite firmly were she to have a choice between him and Sir Marcus, she would choose Sir Marcus, he did not think there was much chance of that.

So he wandered aimlessly around the grounds of the castle, and was quite surprised to run into Emily, on a similar solitary ramble. He asked if he might join her, and she acquiesced, but any harmony between them was quickly squashed when he asked bitterly if he should wish her happy.

"I beg your pardon?"

"You must have realized Sir Marcus would have taken me into his confidence. He told me he was going to propose to you."

"I see," Emily replied, but made no other comment.

"Is it to be a secret engagement then?" Alexander asked, wondering why she persisted in torturing him.

"You are mistaken. Sir Marcus did not propose to me."

"He did not propose? But I was quite sure that was his intention."

"Oh, I am sure it was, also, but that was before he discovered me to be lacking in delicacy." Emily looked up at Alexander, the picture of disappointment, but Alexander saw the laughter lurking in her eyes, and he felt as if a huge weight had been lifted off of him, allowing him to breathe freely.

"I am certain he is right, but may I ask how he made such a discovery?"

Emily looked at him in mock reproach. "You gentlemen are quite ungallant, accusing me of such a thing. If you must know, it is because I laughed in the middle of his marriage proposal. No one had ever informed me of the vulgarity of such behavior. I am sure it was not even discussed at the Bellingham Ladies Academy. Now that I am aware of it, however, I will be sure to attend to my next proposal with the gravity of a pallbearer."

"You may not be the recipient of many more proposals if word gets out of your flighty manner of receiving them." Alexander said, smiling.

"That is true. However, I am not interested in receiving *many* more proposals."

Before Alexander could reply to this auspicious remark, they were met by Lydia and Sedgewick, who
wished they had jumped into the moat before interrupting such a promising tête-à-tête. However, as Lady
Smithfield was ready to return home, they had little
choice but to encourage Emily and Alexander to rejoin
the rest of the party.

એ૦બ

Emily waited in vain for her mother to remark on
her rash behavior of the other night. She was quite surprised when, on Wednesday, her mother had still not
said anything on the subject. Emily was further surprised
to discover that, rather than Lady Smithfield's being angry with her, she had never been so high in her mother's
esteem. She could not understand why her mother was in
such a pleasant mood, particularly as her hopes for Lydia
had not been realized.

On Wednesday morning, the day of Lady Abernathy's ball, Emily was the astonished recipient of a new
ball gown. A pretty, pale jonquil silk, with shoes to
match. The dress had short, puffed sleeves, and a low,
wide neckline, with a darker yellow slip to be worn un-
derneath. Lydia also received a new gown, and both girls
accepted the gifts with such exclamations of delight that
Lady Smithfield was quite pleased with the success of
her surprise.

When the girls came down the stairs that evening,
and Lady Smithfield saw them, she felt like she could
cry, and it was only the thought of how crying always
ruined her complexion that kept any actual tears from
falling. Lydia was always beautiful, of course, but tonight

she glowed with happiness, and the blue dress her mother had chosen for her perfectly matched her eyes. Emily, too, now that she had attracted the notice of Lord Wesleigh, was seen by her mother in an entirely different light. The looks that had before seemed somewhat common were now quite the opposite, as a gentleman who had withstood all the conventional beauties had been captured by Emily's unique beauty.

The duke, who had been waiting with their mother at the foot of the stairs, also thought both girls in exceptional looks. "I will be the envy of every gentleman in the room when I enter the ball with such lovely ladies," he told them. Lady Smithfield felt all the glory of having a ducal escort to the ball, and only wished Sir Marcus could have fit in their carriage as well. However, Sir Marcus, who was avoiding Emily as much as possible since the previous day's debacle, had already left for the ball.

They were received very graciously at Rothergate, which Lady Smithfield correctly attributed to the presence of the duke in their party. Lord Abernathy, to his wife's extreme displeasure, complimented Emily and Lydia on their appearance and warned Lady Cynthia, who was also in the receiving line, that she had some fierce competition. Lady Cynthia did not comment, but only looked Emily and Lydia up and down with an expression of disdain, as if to say she was not too worried.

As the Smithfield party was among the last to arrive, the first set of dances was soon forming. Emily, who had danced the first dance with Lord Farnwright, while the duke had danced with Lady Abernathy, was very gratified when the duke led her out for the second dance. She was not as pleased, however, to see Lady Cynthia join their set with Lord Wesleigh, a smug smile on her aristocratic face.

They were soon observed to be flirting outrageously, which Emily tried her best to ignore. The duke, however, could not figure out what his son was doing flirting with that supercilious blond girl. Did he not tell his father only a week ago that he was in love with Emily Smithfield? "I should have drowned him at birth," the duke muttered under his breath.

Emily, although depressed by Alexander's attention to Lady Cynthia, thought that he might perhaps ask her for the next dance, but as soon as the dance was over he escorted Lady Cynthia to the refreshment room.

Emily, though quite upset, resolved to think no more about it, and smiled brilliantly upon the young man whom Sedgewick was bringing to meet her. The young man, who was introduced as Mr. Henry Watkins, was so struck by the brilliance of Emily's smile that it was not until Sedgewick reminded him of his purpose in approaching Emily that he managed to stammer out a request for the next dance.

Emily agreed, and they took their places in the country dance. Mr. Watkins was a very young man, fresh out of Oxford, who, as a younger son, was destined for the army or the clergy, though at the present could not decide which he preferred. All of this, and more, Emily learned whenever the steps of the dance brought them together. Mr. Watkins's father owned a small farm in Sussex, and he even disclosed the type of cattle that was bred there, although Emily would have been hard put to tell anyone, if asked, what type it was. For, although she gave every appearance of hanging upon his every word, she had stopped listening as soon as Lord Wesleigh and Lady Cynthia reentered the ballroom.

She saw Sedgewick approach Alexander and engage him in conversation, and, as they appeared to be looking in her direction, she began laughing hysterically, as if Mr. Watkins had just been saying something horribly amusing, when in reality he had been describing a horse he had recently purchased.

He looked at her in surprise, and she apologized, but told him what he said had reminded her of a funny incident with a horse when she was a child. To her dismay, he insisted she share the story with him, and she was forced to make something up that was not funny in the least, but to which Mr. Watkins laughed heartily, and said, "By Jove, that's the funniest story I've ever heard."

She would not have been laughing had she overheard Sedgewick's conversation with Alexander. It had begun innocently enough, but as Alexander was desperate to know the name of the gentleman with whom Emily was dancing, and Sedgewick just as eager to tell him, the pleasantries were soon dispensed with and the significant part of the conversation began.

"I do not recognize the young man dancing with Miss Emily Smithfield," Alexander mentioned, in a casual manner.

"That's Mr. Henry Watkins from Sussex. Rather nice chap, actually. Quite taken with Emily. He practically begged me for an introduction."

"They seem to be getting along rather well," said Alexander, having just observed Emily laughing enthusiastically in response to a remark of her partner's. (The remark having to do with the purchase of a new horse.)

"Yes, they do. If I were interested in Emily at all, romantically, I mean, I would be a trifle worried."

Alexander raised his eyebrows at this blatant hint. "Then it's a good thing, I suppose, that you are engaged to Miss Lydia Smithfield and not her sister," he said sardonically.

"Yes, it is a good thing. However, other gentlemen, who are not engaged, may lose out on the opportunity altogether." Mr. Watkins's loud laughter in response to Emily's made-up story punctuated Sedgewick's remark.

"Oh, I am not so sure. Mr. Watkins is only a plain mister after all, and not, I assume, very plump in the pocket."

"He has a comfortable allowance," Sedgewick replied, not knowing if it was true or not but, realizing he had picked rather a poor candidate for jealousy, felt it was his duty to make Watkins look as good as possible.

"Comfortable is not good enough, my friend. Not for Emily Smithfield."

Sedgewick wished to rush to Emily's defense, but they were interrupted at that point by Lady Cynthia, who complained of the heat. Alexander immediately offered to escort her to the gardens, where some fresh air might revive her. Sedgewick watched the scene with much agitation and went to consult with Lydia about what they should do now that their initial scheme had failed.

§)CR

The evening that had so promising a beginning was rapidly turning into the most horrid evening of Lady

Smithfield's recollection. Lady Abernathy had congratu-
lated her on Lydia's engagement, barely concealing her
smirk of triumph. "I assume that there will be no notice
in the *Morning Post* of her engagement to Lord
Wesleigh, now that she's engaged to Mr. Sedgewick,"
she said, laughing at her poor attempt at humor. Lady
Abernathy was so unused to laughing that the sound that
issued from her mouth was more of a bray than an actual
laugh. Lady Smithfield felt it the most unpleasant sound
she had ever heard.

"No, of course not. Although Lord Wesleigh was, of
course, anxious to fulfill his father's wishes, when we observed how attached Lydia was to Mr. Sedgewick, we
could not permit the engagement to proceed, after all."
Lady Smithfield had been amazed when neither Lord
nor Lady Abernathy had seen in Lord Wesleigh a resem-
blance to a certain curate. However, Lord Abernathy was
a trifle shortsighted, and too vain to wear spectacles, and
Lady Abernathy had paid little or no attention to a gentleman she had assumed was far beneath her notice. So
they had merely proclaimed themselves delighted to meet
Lord Wesleigh when introduced to him earlier in the
evening, with never a mention of having met him last
week at Lady Smithfield's dinner party.

"Then I imagine we will soon see another engagement announced," Lady Abernathy said, nodding in the
direction of the dancers.

Lady Smithfield did not grasp her meaning at first.
She wondered if Lady Abernathy could possibly be referring to Lord Wesleigh and Emily. But, when she looked
in the direction Lady Abernathy was looking, she saw
Lord Wesleigh and Lady Cynthia dancing together, and

immediately understood what Lady Abernathy was implying.

Lady Smithfield wanted to contradict this pronouncement right away, but there was no denying the couple appeared very familiar, Lord Wesleigh's dark head bent intimately over Lady Cynthia's fair one. So she said nothing. However, when the dance had ended, and Lord Wesleigh disappeared into the refreshment room with Lady Cynthia on his arm, her alarm grew. Every minute he was away from the ballroom with that hussy seemed like an hour, and she felt she could not sit still a moment longer. Leaving Lady Abernathy to her triumph, she went to find the duke.

She finally found the duke in the card room, where he had retired after his obligatory dance with Lady Abernathy and his more enjoyable one with Emily. She had to wait impatiently for him to finish his hand, but he was soon finished and, seeing that Lady Smithfield desired a word with him, excused himself from the table.

"What is it?" he asked her, as soon as they had distanced themselves a little from the others in the room.

"Your son is paying most marked attentions to Lady Cynthia Sommers."

"Damn. I beg your pardon, Lady Smithfield, but that boy is enough to try the patience of a saint."

"You do not think he means to propose to Lady Cynthia?" Lady Smithfield asked fearfully.

"That uppity yellow-haired chit? I do not think so. But he'd best be careful, for she means to get a proposal if I know anything about women." He thought a moment in silence, while Lady Smithfield observed him in dismay. "Well, I promised I would not interfere, but he's going to ruin the whole business if he's not careful. I think I'd better have a talk with him."

Lady Smithfield murmured her agreement to this plan, and followed the duke from the card room into the ballroom, where they were treated to the sight of Lord Wesleigh walking through the French doors that led to the gardens, with Lady Cynthia on his arm.

Fourteen

෪෨ඏ

Alexander realized he had made a tactical error the moment he left the ballroom. Lady Cynthia had abandoned her haughty manner completely and was treating him with a flirtatious archness that made him very uncomfortable. His intention had been to use her to make Emily writhe with jealousy, as he had from Sir Marcus's attentions to Emily. However, he had obviously not been thinking very clearly, because it was apparent from the way Lady Cynthia clutched at his arm that she had completely mistook his casual flirtation for something more serious.

"There," he said, barely ten feet from the ballroom. "I am sure you are feeling more the thing now. Let us return to the ballroom." He attempted to steer her in that direction, but she was not as fragile as she looked, and it was plain she had no intention of being led back into the ballroom.

"You are mistaken. I am still quite light-headed," she drawled, laying her head against his arm.

"Then I am sure you must want your aunt. Allow me to fetch her for you," Alexander said, growing more uncomfortable by the second.

"You are not very perceptive this evening. You must be aware that I do not want my *aunt* in the least," Lady

Cynthia replied, glancing up at him through half-closed eyes. She had perfected that look in the mirror, and had found it useful on many occasions to bend a recalcitrant gentleman to her will. Alexander thought she looked as if she had had too much to drink. He was quite relieved to hear that someone had exited the ballroom after them, and turned around quickly to see who it was.

Lady Cynthia, who had been practically reclining on Alexander's arm, was startled when he withdrew his support, and she stumbled. She was quite annoyed when, as she attempted to regain her balance, she accidentally stepped on the flounce of her dress. There was a loud ripping sound, and to make her frustration complete, she looked up from an examination of her dress to see Emily Smithfield grinning at her predicament. While Emily felt sorry that Lady Cynthia had damaged her dress, she had been unable to completely hide her amusement at the sight of the graceful and elegant Lady Cynthia reeling about like a drunken sailor.

Before Lady Cynthia could speak, Alexander hailed Emily and her companion enthusiastically. "Miss Smithfield and, I believe it's Mr. Watkins, is it not? What good luck in running into you like this."

"I believe we have interrupted your, um, conversation," Emily said, her implication plain.

"How astute of you—" Lady Cynthia began, in her haughtiest manner, only to be interrupted by Alexander.

"Nonsense. Your arrival is most fortuitous. Lady Cynthia has had an accident and needs to repair her dress. I am sure she would appreciate it immensely if you would escort her to the cloakroom, Mr. Watkins. I just remembered that I had promised to convey a message to

Miss Smithfield."

Lady Cynthia would have protested, but Alexander practically shoved her at Mr. Watkins, and, as Mr. Watkins had no objections to the scheme, Lady Cynthia found herself being returned to the ballroom by her insignificant escort. Mr. Watkins, who had only five minutes ago lost his heart irrevocably to Emily, decided he had been overly hasty and spent the rest of the evening trailing after Lady Cynthia, much to her dismay.

They were met on their way into the ballroom by Lady Smithfield, the duke, Lydia, and Sedgewick, who were quite surprised, and a little cheered, by the sight of Lady Cynthia and Mr. Watkins together. The group proceeded down the path and very quickly caught sight of Emily and Alexander, standing in the middle of a walk by a statue of a Greek goddess. As Alexander and Emily had not observed them, and none of the party wished to interrupt the couple, they quickly positioned themselves behind some bushes and shamelessly eavesdropped on the conversation.

Alexander was telling Emily in a voice that sounded more like that of an irate parent than a lover that she had some explaining to do.

"I beg your pardon?" Emily said, in her best imitation of Lady Abernathy.

"And so you should. What were you doing walking alone in the gardens with that young puppy?"

"I believe, sir, that you were also walking alone in the gardens with a companion who, if I were to continue your use of animal appellations, I would term a cat."

There was a snicker from one of the bushes, hastily suppressed.

"There is a perfectly reasonable explanation for that, my girl," Alexander said.

"Oh?" Emily asked, and Alexander found himself having to provide an explanation of his behavior, without ever receiving one from Emily.

"It was entirely your fault that I was walking out here with Lady Cynthia."

"Really? And was it my fault as well that she was resting her head on your arm?"

The duke nudged Lady Smithfield, whispering to her that their suspicions of Lady Cynthia were correct, and that she was a hussy of the first order.

"Yes, it was," Alexander replied, folding his arms in front of his chest and looking smug.

"Perhaps I am singularly dull-witted, but I really do not see what your assignation with Lady Cynthia has to do with me."

"It was part of an obvious attempt to make you jealous, and I do not think I flatter myself when I believe that I succeeded."

Emily tried to control the racing of her heart at this leading speech, and hoped she managed to look as cool and collected as Alexander.

"Well? Did I succeed?" Alexander asked, who was not as composed as he appeared.

Emily turned and began walking aimlessly down the path, farther away from the house, much to the dismay of her audience, who scrambled to follow without being observed. She finally stopped and sat on a stone bench that, fortuitously enough, was backed by a hedge. Alexander sat beside her, a little closer than she thought was safe, as she felt there was some danger of her poor beleaguered heart jumping out of her chest.

"Emily," Alexander said, in a wheedling tone, as he took her hand in his, "you still have not given me an answer."

"I will admit to being a little jealous," Emily said, too shy to meet Alexander's eyes, "if you tell me to what purpose you tried to make me so."

"I already made that plain, I thought, when I offered for you a few days ago. Perhaps I am foolish to think that your feelings have undergone any change since then."

"No, they have not."

"I see," Alexander said, dropping Emily's hand.

"I love you as much now as I did then," Emily replied softly.

It took Alexander a few minutes to react to this statement, as he was nearly incapable of assimilating such a declaration. When he finally realized what she had said, he turned to her in disbelief. "Then why, my girl, did you refuse me? Didn't you love me enough to marry me believing me to be a curate? I would have married you had you had been a scullery maid in your mother's house."

"I do not believe that."

"Well, maybe not a scullery maid, but had we both been as poor as church mice, I would have still married you, even if we had to wait years before it was possible. I cannot believe that you did not feel the same."

"I did not refuse you because you were a curate. Believe me, if I had thought you to be something as respectable as a curate, I would have accepted you gladly."

"I do not understand. What did you think me to be

if not what I said I was?"

"I thought . . ." Emily paused, and looked away, unable to meet his eyes. "I thought you were the highwayman," she said finally, so softly that Alexander was not sure he had heard her correctly.

"Did you say you thought I was the highwayman?" Alexander asked incredulously, to the satisfaction of his audience, who had been unable to hear Emily's remark and were pleased to have it repeated.

Emily nodded, looking up at him to observe his reaction. To her relief, he appeared more amused than angry.

"Is that why you asked all those questions about the source of my income?" he asked, smiling.

"Yes. And you must admit I had reason to be suspicious. You were attempting to hide your identity as Lord Wesleigh, and, as it was obvious you were hiding something, and I had no way of knowing you were really Lord Wesleigh, I assumed you were someone else. The only person I knew of whose identity was as yet undiscovered was the highwayman. I think it was a very logical conclusion to arrive at, under the circumstances," Emily said defensively.

"My poor girl," Alexander said, putting one arm around her and squeezing her gently. "You must have had a horrible time of it, and all the while I was accusing you of being heartless and mercenary."

Emily just nodded her head, which had somehow found its way under his chin, to rest on his chest. "It's all my fault for being such a romantic fool," Alexander told her. "I wanted to know that you loved me for myself and were not just interested in my fortune."

"Why, if that were all I was interested in, I would

have made up to Sir Marcus while he was posing as you."

"You forget, I accused you of that as well. And if you did not make up to him, why did he propose to you?"

"I have no idea. It came as a complete surprise to me."

They sat quietly for a few minutes, enjoying the comfort of their embrace, while Alexander thought over the events of the past week in the light of this new information.

"So why did you follow Sir Marcus and me the night we went to catch the highwayman?"

"I had to convince myself my suspicions about you were correct. I thought you were out on another stealing spree."

"With Sir Marcus?"

"I did not quite understand why he was present, and hoped that it signified I had made a mistake about you. Or, alternatively, I thought he might have been joining you for a lark."

"Why did you not tell me after I rescued you that you had thought me the highwayman?" Alexander asked.

"I was afraid you would be horribly insulted. I did not realize you would think it so amusing, or you may be sure I would have told you immediately. However, after I found out the next day that you were actually Lord Wesleigh, I deeply regretted not telling you of my suspicion. I thought that you would never believe me after that, suspecting me of lying because I wished to marry you for your fortune."

"And do you?"

"Do I what?"

"Wish to marry me, for any reason other than my fortune."

"Is this a proposal? Because I must say, I enjoyed your first one far more, even when I suspected you of being a highwayman. And Sir Marcus, although he got a bit off the subject, interspersed his insults with a few compliments as well." Alexander did not answer, intent instead on kissing the spot on her shoulder where he had been watching a curl bounce the last ten minutes. Emily, although pleasantly diverted by the tingle down her spine, was distracted by some noises that appeared to be issuing from the bushes to her left. She thought she heard someone complaining that they could not see what was happening, and opening her eyes, she saw her mother's head appear from around the hedge. At first she was embarrassed to have been observed by her mother in a gentleman's embrace, but as the duke and then Lydia and Sedgwick joined her mother, she began giggling. Alexander, oblivious to everything but his rising passion, looked at Emily in disapproval.

"You promised me, my girl, that you would attend to your next proposal with the gravity of a pallbearer," he reminded her.

"Forgive me, my lord," she replied demurely, "but once again the Bellingham Ladies Academy has failed me."

"In what respect?" Alexander asked, a little impatiently.

"They failed to instruct me on the proper way to react when embracing a gentleman and then discovering my entire family observing me from behind a hedge."

"What are you talking about?" Alexander asked, and Emily told him to take a look behind him. He did, and saw his father, Lady Smithfield, Lydia, and Sedgewick standing there, all of them looking a little sheepish. His father was the first to regain his savoir-faire and, approaching his son, asked if he could be the first one to wish him happy.

"I would be happier were I allowed some privacy with my betrothed, but thank you," Alexander said. "How long have you all been standing there?"

"Only a few seconds," the duke replied.

"Yes, I believe they were behind the hedge before that," Emily said, very tongue-in-cheek.

Lady Smithfield felt the wisest course would be to change the subject, and ran to embrace her daughter. "Emily, I could not be happier for you," she said, pulling her up from the bench. Alexander rose as well, and found himself being clapped on the back by Sedgewick.

"Congratulations, old man. It appears we're going to be brothers."

There was an excited jabber of congratulations, and questions about who would be married first and where, while Alexander and Emily exchanged a look of disbelief. It appeared no one was going to offer an explanation for the family's presence behind the hedge.

"Excuse me," Alexander said, cutting into all the babble. "While Emily and I are overjoyed that we have everyone's approval of our engagement, we feel that an explanation is in order."

There was a long silence, while all in the group stared guiltily at the ground, and then the duke spoke. "I know I promised not to interfere, but, dash it all, you were sniffing around that yellow-haired chit like a dog in heat. Didn't want you making a mull of everything."

"And Lady Abernathy implied that your engagement to Lady Cynthia was imminent. If that had occurred, I would never have been able to hold my head up again," Lady Smithfield chimed in.

"Don't see what you have to complain about," Sedgewick said, huffily. "You and Emily meddled in *our* courtship enough."

"We only wanted to see you happy," Lydia added.

"Well I, for one, am quite pleased at your interference," Emily announced into the slight pause that had occurred after the rush of excuses.

"You are?" Alexander asked.

"I am. Knowing your propensity for assuming false identities and leading innocent females on to expect marriage, I am quite relieved that there were witnesses to your proposal. There will be no weaseling out of this engagement, my lord," Emily said sternly.

Oblivious of his audience, Alexander caught Emily up in his arms and kissed her soundly. "The same holds true for you, my girl. No throwing me over for Mr. Watkins, or some other young puppy."

Emily sighed, and attempted to look sorrowful. "But he tells the most amusing stories about horses," she said, and began giggling.

೮೦೧೪

While the engagement had not yet been formally announced, it was pretty well acknowledged when Emily and Alexander returned to the ballroom and danced every dance together. It was also impossible for Lady

Smithfield to keep the news to herself, and Lady Abernathy was among the first to know. Lady Cynthia realized Alexander was a lost cause, and, as Sir Marcus was the second wealthiest man in the room, began flirting outrageously with him. Sir Marcus was able to palm her off on Mr. Watkins for a dance, and tracked down Alexander and Emily in the refreshment room.

"Alex, there you are. You've got to help me, old boy. Lady Cynthia won't leave me alone," Sir Marcus said plaintively, running his finger around his cravat in his anxiety. It was obvious he was laboring under a strong emotion, as he had ruined the perfection of its folds with that unconscious gesture.

"I wish I could help you, Marcus, but I do not see what I can do. You are clearly irresistible."

"You could pay a little attention to her yourself," Marcus suggested.

"I am sorry, but I am already engaged," Alexander replied, gesturing at Emily, who stood a little to one side, to allow the gentlemen their privacy. However, she could still hear everything that was being said.

"I thought I heard a rumor to that effect," Marcus said. "Are you sure you know what you're about?" he whispered quite audibly. "She looks demure enough, but I have reason to know she can be the very devil when she wants to be."

Alexander struggled with a reply, and Emily gave up pretending not to listen. "I am sorry, Sir Marcus, but you are too late," she told him, moving to take Alexander's arm.

"What's that?"

"I have witnesses, you see. He cannot renege on his

proposal."

Sir Marcus looked with pity at Alexander, who was attempting to control his mirth. "I see. I thought it was Lady Cynthia you were after, or I would have warned you." He returned to the ballroom, leaving Emily and Alexander by themselves.

"I still do not understand whatever prompted Sir Marcus to propose to me in the first place," Emily said in wonder, when she had stopped laughing.

"After further thought on the matter, I believe that is my fault. I suggested to Marcus that you preferred him to me. Which you yourself said, if you recall."

"I do not remember saying anything of the sort," Emily replied.

"Emily! You most definitely said it. When I proposed to you in the drawing room of your mother's house. You said if you had to choose between him and me, you would choose him."

"I believe I said he would be the *wiser* choice. But then, I have never been known for my wisdom, or I would never have fallen in love with a penniless curate in the first place."

"No, that would not have been wise, had I in fact been a penniless curate. Neither was it wise on my part to fall in love with a devilish, headstrong girl who will torment me all of our lives."

Emily, although she did not have the benefit of Lady Cynthia's experience in front of the mirror, was able to pout quite enchantingly, which she proceeded to do. Alexander was unable to resist the temptation of those puckered lips, and, looking around the refreshment room to ensure they had no audience, dropped a quick kiss on them. When Emily reached up and pulled him closer, Alexander realized his lifetime of torment had already begun.

Suzanne Allain finds author bios as tedious to write as they are to read. She doubts you *really* want to know where she lives, how many husbands/pets/kids she has, or other careers she dabbled in before striking it rich (or not) as a novelist. However, if you do want to know more about her you can visit: www.suzanneallain.com.

(Answers to items above: husbands: 1, pets: 1, kids: 0)